GOLD IN THEM TEXAS HILLS

An Al Quinn Novel

RUSS HALL

Gold in Them Texas Hills
An Al Quinn© Novel
Red Adept Publishing, LLC
104 Bugenfield Court
Garner, NC 27529
https://RedAdeptPublishing.com/
Copyright © 2025 by Russ Hall. All rights reserved.

Cover Art by Streetlight Graphics[1]

No part of this book may be reproduced, scanned, or distributed in any printed or electronic form without permission. Please do not participate in or encourage piracy of copyrighted materials in violation of the author's rights. Thank you for respecting the hard work of this author.

This is a work of fiction. Names, characters, places, and incidents either are the product of the author's imagination or are used fictitiously, and any resemblance to locales, events, business establishments, or actual persons—living or dead—is entirely coincidental.

---

1.   http://StreetlightGraphics.com

Chapter One

In the corner of the bedroom, Tanner lifted his head and growled, low and steady at first then gradually louder.

Al Quinn's eyes had already snapped open before the dog's warning. He'd sensed something.

Tanner's muzzle might have turned nearly all white in the time since Al rescued him from a scheduled euthanasia at a pet shelter, but his senses hadn't dimmed, nor his tendency to be alert and defensive. This was his family and his home too.

Fergie stirred and rose up on her side of the bed, with the coverlet pulled up to her chin. "What is it?"

"I don't know yet," Al said. "I hope it's just Tanner's stomach kicking up from that half of a burrito he gobbled down when no one was looking."

As he headed to the window, he was thinking, *You get to where you just want to be left the hell alone.* He'd thought theirs was the sort of life that would ensure them being left alone or at least ignored. He, Fergie, and his brother Maury were all in their sixties. Bonnie, at twenty years younger than Maury, had managed to have a child, Little Al, now two years old. It had been months since anything had yanked them from the calm, soothing quiet of their house on the shore of Lake Travis. And that last outing had damn near killed them all.

He pulled aside the curtain and looked out the window. Nothing. He almost let it fall back into place but saw the flicker of a light, the beam of someone's flashlight swinging for a moment across the trunks and lower limbs of trees. "Well, dammit, Janet."

Al dropped the curtain back into place and rushed to his gun cabinet and dialed in the combination. They had just gotten back to such an aura of peace that he no longer kept a pistol in the bedside stand or in his glove box in the truck. Tanner got up onto all fours and started to lumber toward the bedroom door.

Fergie threw off the covers and scrambled naked out of bed. Her long red hair whipped out as she grabbed her jeans, tugged them on, and slid her bare feet into her boots. In the brief glances he got of her nude, he appreciated once again how fit and lean she had remained, years after they once jointly experienced the worst prom date ever, only to come together and get married at last, only a short while back.

Al pulled on his shirt, jeans, and boots. Holding his Sig Sauer in his right hand, he headed out into the house to peer out the back windows, which looked over the two tiers of the backyard that led down to the lake's shore.

He saw the flickering light more clearly. *Definitely a flashlight,* he thought.

Fergie came to stand beside him. She held her Glock in her right hand down at her side. "What is it?"

"Someone's down there, nosing about with a light." He glanced at his watch and saw it was a little past three in the morning.

Bam!

"Now what?" Fergie spun and ran beside Al as they both tried to go down the stairs to the lower floor's back door at the same time, bumping shoulders and elbows all the way. Fergie was taller than Al at six foot three and faster, so he was the one struggling to keep up by the time they got to the bottom.

Maury was standing by the bed he shared with Bonnie. He was holding Little Al to his chest. "She's out there," he said, nodding toward the open back door. "She got her peashooter from under her pillow and was out the door like scalded lightning."

"Take him upstairs," Al said. "The gun safe is open. Get the Model Twelve out for yourself, and stay up there until you hear from us."

Fergie got out the back door first, but Al was right behind her. A cement walk went to a set of stairs, going down to another walk then another staircase to get down to the lake level with the boathouse and fishing dock. A gust of wind tugged at his hair, and he caught just a faint hint in the breeze that, at least a half mile away, a skunk was moving about in the night air.

Bam! Bam!

Al gripped the pistol more tightly and ran faster. But Fergie's long legs and regular training put her in the lead.

This is one hell of a nighttime activity for two folks in their sixties, Al thought as he ran. He could smell the lake's water and catch glimpses of the moon slipping in and out of shredded rags and wisps of clouds.

As they scrambled down the second set of cement stairs, a boat's motor started. Outlined against the glow of moonlight on the water's surface, Bonnie stood a level up from the boat dock in her robe, short and chunky with the hand holding her Chiefs Special still in the air.

A boat took off as fast as it could go, swerving a bit at first as the driver struggled for control. It spread out a wide silver wake as it roared away until it was soon out of sight.

Bonnie lowered the gun she held as she turned to them. "I just fired a couple of warning shots and aimed so the lead would fall out into the lake, away from any houses or people."

"Any idea what they were up to?" Fergie asked.

"I didn't ask, and they didn't say," Bonnie said. "But here. I'll show you something."

The sound of the departing boat was long gone as Al and Fergie followed Bonnie almost to the house, where she pointed down at a spot on the ground. She hadn't used a flashlight to find the spot, having spent years in the dark following her daddy on coon hunts in the middle of the night. She had learned to shoot with a marksman's skill as well as see in the dark during those outings.

As soon as they were up to where she stood, Al saw a metal detector lying on the ground where someone had dropped it as soon as any shooting had begun.

"Maury's been wanting one of these," Bonnie said.

"Looks like he's got one unless those jaspers come back after it," Fergie said.

"That doesn't seem likely since Bonnie just put a tickle of fear up their spines," Al said. "But all the same, I think we'd better keep a watch for a spell. You two go back to bed. I'll take the first shift."

"Naw. I'll be inside, making a pot of coffee," Bonnie said. "And I'll bring you a mug first thing." She bent to pick up the metal detector. "At the least, I'll get this out of the way so Maury can mess around with it, come daylight. This is just the sort of thing that'll perk him up, especially if he has a chance to find gold or something."

"I doubt that'll happen. All the gold that's ever been found in the state of Texas in all the years is just a tad over eight thousand ounces," Al said. He was the most avid historian of them.

"Mind you, that was back in the eighteen hundreds, when gold was worth just a bit over twenty dollars an ounce," Fergie said. "That'd be about five hundred dollars' worth then, a good sixteen million now, with gold at nearly two thousand an ounce."

Al raised an eyebrow at her. "Someone's been having a poke at my history books."

Fergie grinned. "It's been quiet around here, a good time for reading... Until now."

She and Bonnie turned to head up to the house.

"I'll bring you that mug of coffee," Bonnie called back over her shoulder.

As the quiet settled back over the area around him, Al relaxed to the sound of waves hitting the shore and the leaves rustling high in the trees from a breeze coming in off the water. He chuckled silently to himself.

Gold! The closest found near where I live was in the Llano Valley and the rest way the hell out west near Presidio and Hazel.

So the visit by whoever it had been in the night might have been about several things, but he doubted very much it had anything to do with gold.

Chapter Two

The horizon to the east was gradually shifting from a whitish glow to orange with tinges of red when Al heard footsteps coming down the cement stairs that led down from the house. He sat in an Adirondack chair facing the lake. All night he'd sat with the rifle across his lap, listening to every shore-slapping wave of water, each bird chirp, and the strange rustling of leaves pushed around in the treetops by wind. For the life of him, he still hadn't figured out why anyone would want to sneak around on his property in the dark.

"Coming to have a turn watching nothing happening all at once?"

Fergie came around where he could see her. "Do you think anyone will be bold or crazy enough to come at us when it's daylight?"

"Nope. Well, probably not. But with people these days, who knows?"

She picked up his empty mug and nodded toward the scoped 30-06 rifle he held, which Bonnie had brought down to the shoreline along with the coffee. "Come up to the house and grab a nap with Tanner. He's camped out at the foot of your bed, pining away for you."

Al stood up and stretched. "They might come back to finish what they were trying to start or at least get their toy back."

"They'll have to pry it out of Maury's sweaty paws. He's been like a kid at Christmas with the damned thing, and he says it's no toy."

They started up the steps together. As they crested the set of steps that took them to the level of the lower floor's back door, Al heard Maury.

"Another blankety-blank can tab." Maury shook his head but nevertheless tucked the metal bit into a plastic bag that hung from his belt.

He wore jeans and a safari shirt open over a wifebeater shirt, with the strap of the metal detector over his shoulder.

"You'll not get rich that way," Al said.

Maury looked up from the ground at them. "Not at fifty cents a pound for the damn things. But I have to get the lawns clear of these and bottle caps before I can get a clear reading on anything like a treasure."

"Who says there's a treasure?" Al went closer to take a look at the metal detector Maury held.

Fergie signed to Al that she was going inside. She took the rifle he held out to her and headed for the back door, slipping in quietly in case Little Al was still asleep this early.

Al glanced up at the sky, which was a brighter white and would soon be blue. The day was warming up and would get a whole lot hotter once the sun was all the way up.

"This thing I'm holding tells me someone was serious." Maury held it up so that Al could see the brand markings. "You can buy metal detectors for anywhere from thirty dollars to three hundred. But for a Minelab Equinox in this model, the nine hundred, you'd pay around thirteen hundred dollars. Someone wanted to use the good stuff. I'd kind of like to know why."

"I'd rather know whether they intend to show up again and try to get it back," Al said. "I thought we were over the days of having to do night patrols and stand watches. You haven't beeped onto anything of significant value, have you?"

"I found a couple of things. Someone put seventeen pennies into a leather pouch and lost it near a pecan tree's trunk. I like to think some child was saving to get the parents something nice for Christmas then lost the savings."

"Even back in the day, I doubt you could buy much with that kind of loot."

"Well, they were wheat pennies. But that was probably common back then. Still, I feel bad for the kid. Plus, I found the setting to a ring. The stone is missing, and I doubt it's real gold. Nevertheless, a find. There's something else. Follow me."

With the detector held loose in one hand as it swung on its strap, Maury trudged up the hill that ran along the side of the house so that both the back door and the front door of the upper floor opened at ground levels.

"Up here, over by that mesquite tree. Take a look."

Al moved closer and saw a pile of twenty or so dirt-covered horseshoes beside three large metal hoops.

"The metal rings went around wagon wheels," Al said. "The shoes are probably from when this property was a stop on the stagecoach line."

"When I found these things"—Maury waved a hand at the piles of metal—"the detector went off so loud it about blew off my ears. It sounded like Fort Knox. For just a tiny stretch there, I really was thinking I might've tumbled onto some gold. But no, just a tiny piece of Wild West history."

"Stagecoaches ran along lines with stations about a hundred and sixty miles apart where they could switch out to get four fresh horses and maybe a bite of some pretty bad grub."

"Whee. Pretty heady stuff. Did they haul around gold or treasures much?"

"Only in the dime novels, the kind Ned Buntline wrote."

Maury twisted left and right, stretching himself. "Want to stay out with me and see what else I find with this thing?" He grinned.

"Nope. I'll let you have all the fun while I catch up on sleep. I imagine you went right back to bed after your Annie Oakley wife was done shooting up Dodge City."

"Of course I did."

"Well, later then." Al headed for the front door, already picturing himself slipping between the comfy covers of his bed.

AL WENT INTO THE BEDROOM, and Tanner's head rose. When he saw it was Al, he rose slowly, came over, and rubbed his side against Al's leg while Al was unbuttoning his shirt. He glanced over, and Fergie was taking off her boots.

"What're you doing?"

"You're not just gonna get in there by yourself?" Fergie's grin looked a little wicked or at least sultry.

"I was thinking that."

Tanner moved over to curl up close to the head of the bed on Al's side.

"Don't you think you might need help with relaxing?" She winked.

"Well, yes. Now that you mention it, I might. You want to talk awhile?"

"No. I'm more in the mood to cut to the chase."

"Then cut to the chase it is." Al slid naked into bed, and Fergie did the same from her side.

They'd never shared any hot teenage moments together, but they made up for it in that moment, which was as peppery as being in the back seat at some drive-in movie.

MAURY HAD WATCHED AL go to the front door and slip inside. He should have brought out the dog, Tanner, so he'd have someone to talk to and share in his treasure-hunting adventure. He liked being out in the smell of the woods with the sound of trucks going past on the road just on the other side of a thick stand of trees. He was wondering if the old stagecoach route had gone by right where he was standing. Maury thought it likely the stage's relay station, stables, and maybe even a blacksmith shop were located farther back, near where he'd found all the horseshoes. Then he got a beeping, a really sudden and loud beeping. He'd acquired some kind of a target. That got all his attention. He bent closer to the ground over the spot that had made all the noise, trowel in hand, not hearing the soft footsteps of someone running up behind him.

A hand went around his face, palm covering his mouth to prevent a scream or yell, while the thumb and forefinger pinched his nose, cutting off all air.

He tried to think of and do the things he'd seen Al do, kicking back, twisting, and throwing the guy over his shoulder. A big arm held Maury's arms to his sides and pressed him toward the ground. The guy felt like a truck weighing Maury to the earth. Bits of dirt, sand, gravel, and grass pressed against his knees then his chest as all that weight pressed harder and heavier.

Maury tried to swing his arms, but those gripping arms held his in place. Someone else held his legs at the ankles. He couldn't see who was behind him, but there were two of them, and both were stronger than he was. Not all that long ago, he'd had a heart attack, which was how Bonnie came to be his nurse. He sincerely hoped he wasn't going to have another one or die. That was the last scrap of thought he had as everything grew black.

BONNIE FUSSED OVER Little Al and got him into his shorts, shoes, and a T-shirt that read Center of the Universe.

"I don't know where your father has gotten to. We'll have to go after him. He's got a new toy, and he won't have the sense to come in for lunch with that blasted thing in his hands."

"Daddy? Toy?" Little Al clapped his hands.

Surprisingly, Maury had turned into the best kind of a father for their two-year-old son. But Bonnie would give him his moment. A new shiny object had fallen into his hands.

"Well, let's go get him." Bonnie lifted the boy up and held him against her chest.

Once out the front door, she put Little Al down on the ground and held him by the hand.

"Squir'l."

"No, that was a lizard. Hear it scampering away among the dry leaves. You're a giant to it."

"Gi'nut."

Bonnie had her Chiefs Special tucked into her waistband but didn't think she'd need it in the bright daylight. Still, she peered into the woods around them with the sharp eyes of someone who had done a whole lot of hunting with her pappy in her youth.

The lane curved around a stand of sumac that had been blocking her view, and she saw a body stretched out on the ground ahead. Those were Maury's clothes.

She screamed and scooped up Little Al and went running over to Maury.

"Whee!" Little Al waved his arms.

Bonnie looked around carefully as she put the boy down to stand on the ground. She reached toward Maury with a shaking hand, felt his pulse, and gave a huge sigh.

Maury's face was flushed, and the metal detector was gone. She stood and peered all around again then reached for her phone.

When Fergie answered, Bonnie said, "If you two are done doin' the horizontal mambo, you'd better hustle up here to the front of the property. Someone's roughed up Maury and taken away his new toy."

"Toy?" Little Al said.

Chapter Three

Maury was sitting up with his back to the bole of a pecan tree when Al and Fergie came jogging up to where Bonnie was tending to him while holding Little Al with one hand. Both of them held a pistol in one hand and looked about as they ran.

"I think whoever did this is as gone as bell-bottom pants." Bonnie waved a hand toward Maury. "He's lucky to be alive. They cut off his air for a spell."

Al bent down on one knee close to his brother Maury. "You okay?"

"I've been better." He brushed a hand through his hair. "They took all the stuff I'd found as well as the detector, Al. Had to be the same people."

"I don't know what's going on with the world that we can't be left the hell alone," Al said. "We're out here in as faraway bum-fart nowhere in Texas as can be. What's with everyone?"

"They held me so tight. I tried to fight, but they pinched my nose and covered my mouth until I passed out."

"You're lucky," Fergie said. "That's a dangerous thing to do to anyone. You're just a few ticks more from not being able to wake up again at all."

"Well, I certainly didn't enjoy any part of it." Maury got slowly to his feet with Bonnie helping him and Little Al clinging to one jeans leg. He dusted himself off. "And they got all my stuff as well as the detector. Do you think they'll be coming back?"

"I'm almost certain of it. These are men willing to take big chances, risks, and that hints they think there's a big reward. However deluded they are, we'll have to watch out for them."

"If I get next to them, you just wait." Bonnie's hand reached down to touch the butt of her pistol.

"I think this might be a good time for you, Maury, and the baby to pack up and take a little trip to somewhere safe," Al said.

Bonnie's face rocked back like he'd slapped her. Her eyes narrowed at him. "Are you scared?"

"No. A little ticked off but not scared."

"Well, I'm the same as you. My pappy would curl up like a worm in his grave if he thought I'd skedaddled and missed out on the fun of popping someone."

"That's just it. We don't want you popping anyone. Don't you want Maury and the baby to be somewhere safe?"

"I know that's how you might think, but we've been through worse messes than this, and here we are."

Al glanced toward Fergie. She knew, too, that it was in Bonnie's character to never back down from a scrap. She'd always been that way, and they couldn't expect her to change. Bonnie was also the youngest of them, and the best shot, even though Fergie was a retired city police detective and Al was the same after his thirty years of detective days on the sheriff's department.

Maury was rubbing his neck along his shirt collar, but he nodded.

"Pop. Mom pop." Little Al formed his little hand into the shape of a gun. "Pop. Pop."

Al knew better than to comment on the way Bonnie was raising her son, even if it looked like he was going to be some sort of a son of a gun.

Chapter Four

Shade from a sycamore tree covered the ground where Fergie sat back in one of the two wooden Adirondack chairs, watching Al standing out in the sun and fishing off the dock. A cool breeze swept across the lake, occasionally tugging at her ponytail. That was just as well since the sun was beating directly down on Al, who wore a ball cap, T-shirt, and jeans. He had a knack for visualizing what was going on with his lure as he reeled it back toward the dock. But at the moment, his eyes were taking in every boat and Jet Ski on the lake. She could sense his unflinching tension and alertness, underscored by the Sig Sauer tucked inside his belt at the small of his back.

Tanner was stretched out on the green Astroturf that covered the dock. As old as he was, he still stared out across the lake as well, alert and keen to be a part of whatever the hell was going on.

"You think they're going to have to come back again, don't you?" she asked.

"I don't think that whatever the hell they were up to is finished. So, yeah. They'll be back. I sure hate that since I was just getting back into the groove of calm days and midday naps."

"We start to sound old when you put it like that."

"We're sure not any kind of young."

"I think having a young child in the house makes me *feel* younger." She realized that had brought a smile to her face.

"It gives us more to protect too. I sure wish Bonnie had just headed for the hills until whatever is going on is over."

"She's up by the road now with the thirty-aught-six, prowling around, and is as happy as a raccoon with a bucket of clams. She eats up what she calls these 'little adventures.'"

An osprey flew by, holding a good-sized bass in its talons, nose forward. It slowed and turned to land on a high bare limb where it could dine in the manner to which it was accustomed.

"Damned thing is showing off," Al muttered.

"Let's be real. You're not really fishing. I saw you shake off something a minute ago that tried to take off with your plastic worm."

"Come to that, you've been sitting kind of gingerly on an otherwise comfortable chair. Could that be because of the gun you have tucked in at the back of your slacks?"

"Could be." She reached to tug out the Glock and put it on the right arm of the chair. She let out a sigh. "When I was still in uniform, we were always hearing how the way you wear your holster could end up pinching your sciatic nerve. Sitting with a gun pressed up against your lower spine isn't a whole heap better."

Someone let out a whoop from the back of a Jet Ski way on the other side of the lake. She watched Al tense for a second. But it was just some tomfool who thought loud was the only way to enjoy a day outdoors.

When she first moved out to the house to live with Al, the lake had called to her morning and night. The gentle, regular waves, each climbing as the wind strummed the surface like a harp, were hypnotic and calming. Breezes rustled the leaves in the trees along the shore, and even when the sun was high in a cloudless blue sky, the water would be cool in spots. Yet when a body was found tucked into an old rusty barrel underwater and when she saw a man's head explode in a spray of blood by a boat ramp, the lake's peaceful quality had taken on an edge. At the moment, she was feeling threatened once again. Someone had roughed up Al's older brother, who was inside now, resting while watching Little Al, a tiny vulnerable being—the most vulnerable of them and needful of the most protection. Fergie wished Bonnie had the sense to just go away and hide, but that wouldn't be Bonnie, who'd grown up hunting with her pappy and could pretty well shoot the eyelashes off a gnat. It wasn't just that she wouldn't want to miss a tussle by going away—it was far bigger than that. To make her go away and hide would be a huge blow to her pride and her entire personality. She was Bonnie to the core, and they might as well beat her with whips as send her packing. They'd just have to keep an extra careful eye on Little Al and Maury, too, for that matter.

"I'd sure like to have back that picture in my head of us just living quietly and peacefully out here by the lake in grace and dignity, not being twitchy and on the prod once again." Al reeled in a small bass, took it off the hook, and eased it back into the water.

"Amen." Fergie had her eye on a boat heading closer, but it was just someone looping back to pick up a water-skier who had dropped into the water like a sack of mail.

A blue heron that had been halfway hiding in reeds a few yards up along the shore took off with wide flapping strokes of its wings and an irritated squawk at the boat it felt had threatened its fishing.

Al made another cast and started to reel in. Fergie leaned her head back against the chair and started to close her eyes.

Snap!

A loud twig broke beneath someone's step behind them.

In what seemed one united movement, Al dropped his rod to the dock. Both he and Fergie spun with their guns pointed at the source of the noise.

There stood Maury holding Little Al's tiny hand as he led him down the hill toward the dock.

Maury froze where he stood, eyes open as wide as they could get. "Sorry," he said. "Did I startle y'all?"

Chapter Five

"What the hell were you thinking? You could have done in that old dude." Griff pressed harder on the accelerator of his 2007 Dodge Ram truck, which was covered and held together mostly by rust, J-B Weld, Bondo, and the red of an $99.95 Earl Scheib paint job not long before they went out of business. He thought that gave the vehicle character, but it also made it easier to identify, which was why he continued to go as fast as he dared on the winding up-and-down two-lane road. A plume of black smoke billowed from his tailpipe. *Damned thing uses as much oil as gas!*

"We got our thing back. Now we can look around there some more." Budge carried the metal detector cradled in his arms like a precious baby, no doubt feeling a little guilty that he'd been the one to drop it and run when some crazy person from the house had started peppering the sky with lead in what they were sure was their direction.

"Just remember that time at the kicker bar." Griff clenched the steering wheel tighter.

A guy in a black cowboy hat with pearl buttons on his plaid shirt had tried to mug Griff in the dark parking lot. Budge had slipped up behind the would-be robber, slapped away the locked-blade knife held in the right hand, and put the same sleeper hold on him, cutting off all air by covering the mouth and pinching the nose. Maybe Budge had held him that way too long. But when Budge let go, the fellow crumpled to the gravel like a bag of sand to land among the broken teeth and broken dreams already lying there. He wasn't breathing. They looked around. No one had seen them. While Budge was clambering into their truck as fast as he could, Griff copped the guy's wallet then got in the truck

"

and drove them briskly away. No good could come from them trying to report some stiff in the parking lot. Explaining such things just gets misunderstood. But that mugger was one fellow who was never going to two-step again.

"You don't think we put those people back there on their guard, made them more alert?" Griff asked. "They seem the sort to take umbrage at trespassers. At least one of them was taking shots at us."

Budge shook his head. With three hundred pounds of mostly gym muscle and sporting a longish dark-brown mullet, he had probably practiced the shake in the mirror, thinking the toss of hair would be chick magnet and a half. Women had not, to his reluctant surprise, come rushing toward him. But Griff left that alone, having seen Budge on one occasion lift one end of a full-sized slate pool table and topple it over onto someone who had laughed at him. Sensitive, that's what he was.

Griff was not above charges of being more than a little vain himself. His father had drummed into his bony young head that if a man looked good, all else would fall into place around that—women, jobs, and even the world's opinion of him. Presenting himself in the appropriate accoutrements to dazzle did not come easily or inexpensively.

He glanced down at his knock-off Rolex Daytona, just like the one Paul Newman had, and Newman's had sold for over fifteen million. The one Griff owned, he had come by on a street corner in Dallas for a crisp one-hundred-dollar bill, grabbed quickly by a guy who swore the watch was real. Griff knew damn well better, but it sure looked good on his wrist and held up to the quick glance of anyone not carrying a jewelry loupe. He didn't mind having to clean off a green spot on his wrist each night. It was part of a step in the right direction, and if his plans came together someday, he would own a real one.

Every item Griff wore was intended to show class and care. Though his clothes did not come from a bespoke tailor on Savile Row but instead represented hours of careful picking at thrift shops, he sported a suede jacket, a clone of Todd Snyder corduroy slacks, and a mock black turtleneck shirt that screamed Steve Jobs. The watch was the eye candy that set it all off.

Someday, everything he wore would be real, but that took money. He had tried everything except honest work. He didn't want to rob banks, like his old man, who had died in the Huntsville prison. What he needed was a get-rich-quick scheme, hence his obsession with gold.

When his Uncle Leo passed away, selfishly taking his iconic gold tooth, which had winked at Griff with every smarmy smile, Griff had showed up at the funeral parlor early.

"Could I have just a moment or two alone with my dear Uncle Leo?" he said as he slipped a folded twenty into the hand of a man who looked like he'd breathed in far too much formaldehyde for far too many years and had a low salary to boot.

Once the door closed behind the employee, Griff whipped out a pair of pliers. It was going to be a closed casket, after all.

But the real opportunity came along when he and Budge drove up to Plano, home to the highest median income in the Dallas area, to attend an estate sale. Griff hoped for an oversight where he could get a steal on an underpriced item. While he tapped on vases and sniffed at oil paintings, Budge was over at a table of books. The damned fool was one hell of a reader.

Griff was looking closely at what he thought was a jade carved dragon on a wooden base that looked to be teak. As soon as he lifted it, he knew it was plastic and thought, *Fake.* He was putting it down when Budge came over with a leather-bound book he said he'd gotten for a dollar.

"Let me see that," Griff said.

Budge handed it over so that Griff could take a closer look at the fore edges of the pages, which looked mottled. Sometimes when bent just right, a painted book edge would show up, and a dollar book could be worth a cool thousand or two. When he held apart the boards of the covers and bent the edges just right, he saw nothing. He handed the book back to Budge, who smiled and held it closely. At times he could be like an eleven-year-old kid unless it came to picking up some dude and tossing him around like a bag of trash.

Where Budge was quick and tough in some ways, he was also soft-hearted in others, kind of a yin to Griff's hard-edged yang. Once, he found a dog chained outside a house without food or water, in the sun, way out in the middle of no damn where. Without Griff knowing about it, he waited for the dog's owner, hit him from behind with a hammer of a fist to the head, dropping him, big as he was, and used chains to fasten the guy to the same tree with no food or water. Then he took the dog to a shelter three counties away. Griff didn't hear about it until at least three days later, when some relative had gone out and found the fellow with his tongue hanging out and damn near dead. When Budge chuckled at the TV news story, Griff got him to admit his hand in it.

"Don't do stuff like that," he told Budge.

"Why? It's what he done to the dog. Fair is fair."

Griff didn't say anything more. But that sort of thing could easily have bounced a murder rap their way. However, the guy did have a bad record for the way he treated dogs, and Griff had doubted the cops even looked for fingerprints. Still and all.

Back in their cheapo motel room, Budge was sprawled in a chair, reading his book, when an envelope fluttered out onto the floor. Griff almost stepped on it as he was going past but picked it up. The envelope looked and felt old and hadn't been opened. Even the stamp was worth something, old as it was, a ten-cent Jefferson brown that had been can-celled, taking its value down to about fifty bucks. An unused mint-con-dition version of the same stamp would have been worth more like fif-teen hundred.

"Hey, I was using that as a bookmark," Budge said.

Griff slit the envelope open with his pocket switchblade and handed the envelope back to Budge. He would get the stamp off later. "Here you go."

He carefully opened the stiff, thin page of the letter and read it.

Dearest Effie,

Don't tell yer Uncle Elrod nothing about this. You know him. Anyways, I got my hands on it, near 42 pounds of gold pulled out of the Franklin Mountains near El Paso's Guadalupe Mission. Took the stage through the Guadalupe Mountains and was comin yer way. But the handles on the carpetbag started pullin lose from the weight. Had to burry it in a scrap heap behind the stagecoach station whilst they was changing horses. Plannin to go back, but I kinduv took a bullet while getting hands on the stuff so if I don't make it you need to go digging behind station 57 along the Colorado just past the ford. Don't tell Elrod.

Luvin you, Heck

Griff had put down the letter and looked off into a corner of the motel room. *Could it be so much hokum? Probably not, though.* It sure felt right.

BUDGE, THE READER OF the two, had put on his best shirt, a silver-and-black Guayabera he'd picked up in Nuevo Laredo, and Griff had driven him to the library, where Budge's laborious due diligence could begin while Griff spent the time flirting unabashedly with a librarian who was never going to see forty again. Griff sure couldn't wait outside in the truck. The day out there in the Texas sun was shaping up to be more than a hundred degrees again at the beginning of what some said was going to be another monster drought. The air was cool and brisk inside the building.

Fortunately for Budge, the library had shelves of books on Texana history. As the saying went, "You can always tell a Texan, but you can't tell him much." Many of them took pride in the state's history, which led to quite a few books and computer files on the subject. Budge had been reluctant at first to believe in a letter that had landed in their laps like it had popped out of a time machine.

He knew that Griff liked to think of himself as the smart one. He was a better dresser—that was for sure. Yet he was nowhere near as big a reader as Budge.

Griff had a degree he carried around to show to others that said he was a graduate of Southeast North Dakota State University. That might fool others, but Budge could account for the time Griff would have been away at a school or even taking remote classes, and that's if the school existed in the first place, which Budge seriously doubted. Griff's diploma hadn't held up to a background check by some overzealous PR intern who seemed to have something to prove. Of course, Griff didn't get the job for which he was applying, but he found out what car the intern drove and had let all the air out of the tires.

Since Griff was his best pal, Budge treaded lightly around the entire subject. He also didn't mind that Griff had dumped the bulk of the research work on him. He liked it. Having his nose in books was like entering a wonderland, one that swept him far away from growing up around people who thought him one of a couple of young thugs. Boy, the two of them had been a pair back then, like the time Budge accidentally broke starting quarterback Ricky Thorton's arm in three places. So Ricky had to sit out the season, picking up splinters in his butt from the bench, while the school's promising year turned into a losing season, and Budge had spent some time in detention. Big deal. No one messed with him there.

Back in high school, Griff had wanted others to call him "Slick." Only Budge, his loyal friend, had gone along with that for the short spell it lasted. But Griff had an edge, a ruthless, almost animal cunning, a con man's eye for how to come out ahead, although at times, that led to him flying off on a tangent. It made Budge cynical about the gist of the letter until he did his own deep digging.

Budge finally felt he had identified the exact stagecoach station he wanted along Lake Travis, which had once been the Colorado River. In the course of his digging, he had learned that 458 stagecoach robberies had taken place between 1856 and 1913, when the railroads took over. But the gold they were after could have come from none of them, which was better, since it could be *all theirs* once they got their hands on it. He had found no other mention of it in all the buried-treasure-in-Texas books he could read either, except that the treasure he was focusing on had not yet been found. He had the inkling of a reason to disagree.

Given everything he could find about where the stagecoach came from, he surmised that the only place where that amount of gold could have originated was from a hidden treasure, not a mine. The main such legend came from the Franklin Mountains and dated from 1595, when Juan de Oñate hid a conquistador treasure of nine burro loads of jewels, four Aztec codices, five silver bars, and 4,336 gold ingots in an abandoned mine. Budge could imagine the conquistador having reason to hide away a pillaged treasure for later. Known for the Acoma massacre, he had killed five hundred warriors as well as three hundred women and children. Then he ordered the right foot chopped off the only surviving twenty-four Acoma warriors. For mismanagement of that Santa Fe de Nuevo México territory, as well as excessive cruelty, he was exiled from New Mexico but probably meant to return for the loot after his trip to Spain to defend himself against violating a royal decree against cruelty to Indians. Some people had been looking for years for the cache he left behind.

Budge was able to confirm that when the Pueblo Indians rose up against their Spanish masters, killing priests and all, a treasure was hidden somewhere in the area. Through the years, many treasure-hunting groups had gone after what came to be known by some as the Lost Padre Mine. But they never found it.

Griff double- and triple-checked on the lost treasure, looking everywhere he could. Such buried treasures were often called by various names, but the letter was the glue that made him believe he was on the track of something real. Everyone thought the hidden treasure in some cave had never been found, but maybe it had, at least part of it. If someone had gotten their hands on at least some of the gold in the cache and had shot this Heck fellow in the process of being robbed, that could explain how a significant amount of gold came to be buried at a stagecoach station as Heck's strength was running out, as well as his luck, perhaps.

Budge had next looked up the value of gold. Forty-two pounds at about two thousand dollars an ounce would be worth somewhere over a million. They had found their opportunity at last.

All that he found and read came to give more strength to the letter telling how someone had spirited away some of the gold and even taken a bullet in the process. He'd come at last to believe in the possibility of their getting rich themselves. He knew there were risks, but so it was with almost anything worth having. Griff and he would get their chances. They just had to figure out how. Now, all they had to do was get back onto that property. The old dude using their detector had covered some ground but not all of it.

Chapter Six

Fergie came out of her bedroom and looked around at the kitchen and living room. She had to admit that the rooms sparkled. Bonnie was futzing around at a countertop between the sink and stove, but she'd clearly had time to clean and had probably thoroughly enjoyed herself while doing so.

Fergie had to suspect that if Al had ended up living alone in the house, as he'd expected, he'd probably have settled for merely keeping it tidy. As a former nurse and conscientious homemaker, Bonnie tended toward polishing, scouring, vacuuming, and constantly cleaning until everything was spic and span.

When the frenzy to clean was upon Bonnie and Fergie or Al offered to help, she would say, "I've got this." Maury knew her well enough to just stay back and out of the way. If cleaning chores was hers to do, part of how she paid her way around the house, then Fergie and Al would let her have that. She even cleaned windows.

"What're you up to?" Fergie glanced Bonnie's way as she went to get a mug out of the cabinet. She took one of Al's old mugs that said Give Peas a Chance, which she knew dated back to the seventies or eighties.

"Just soaking some pinto beans overnight so I can make up a big mess tomorrow."

Tanner pressed against Bonnie's leg and stared up at the ham bone she was unwrapping from the foil around it.

"It's not for you," she told him.

"Tanner's sure interested in the smell of that bone." Fergie filled her mug with coffee from the thermos.

"He'll get the bone once it's been cooked with the beans and the rest of the bits of ham have come off."

"Are you sure a big pot of beans is the best idea with us all cramped up together?"

"It's only a step away to get to the great outdoors, as my pappy used to say." Bonnie tilted her head as she looked up at Fergie. "Do you think being stuck here, having to hang around the house and keep a lookout, amounts to some form of terrorism? I mean these people, whoever they are, they're controlling our actions."

"Are you afraid of them?"

"You know better than that. I ain't afeared of a lot of things that I should be, especially if loved ones are involved. Maybe I was born without fear, like my pappy, nor without too much sense when it comes to danger. I'd wrestle a bobcat if it was coming after Little Al. I don't even know who these guys are or what they look like. But they hurt Maury. Knocked him out. That kind of choking might've killed him, especially after his heart troubles. If they come again, I won't be afraid, but I'll sure be watching with care, mind you."

"I can't imagine who they are or what they're up to either." Fergie took a sip of coffee. "But I'm pissed at them all the same for upsetting the peaceful phase we were in for a while."

Bonnie was just getting out the fixings to make corn bread when Maury's yell sounded from the front door.

"We've got company!" Before they could scramble for their guns, he added, "Not to worry. It's a friend."

Sheriff Clayton held his white cowboy hat in his hand so that he wouldn't have to duck when he came inside the front door. He crossed the room to the kitchen area. He was John Wayne big and looked like he'd grown up wrestling grizzlies. Big as a tree and as weathered as one that'd been through its share of storms, he had the tanned and textured skin of a sequoia, more dried and tough than wrinkled. He'd been sheriff in the county for a long time, a duration that covered a good chunk of Al's thirty years in the department.

Fergie had known the sheriff for years, part of that from her long stint as a detective in the Austin Police Department. Clayton seemed to her one of those sorts of men who could have two or three trains of thought going on in that large head while still appearing to be listening intently.

"I'm curious what brings you out this way." Fergie held out a hand.

"I'm more curious myself about what Maury here was doing by the front end of your drive, toting a shotgun," Clayton said in a voice that boomed inside the room. "It's not any hunting season I know about."

"Depends on what you're hunting," Bonnie said.

"Oh, dear. Has Miss Oakley here been terrorizing the villagers again?"

"More like they've been doing that to us." Bonnie humphed.

"What do you want, Clayton?" Fergie asked. "And can I get you a cup of coffee?"

"I'm here to have a quiet chat with Al. But, yes, I could do with a mug. Bonnie makes a helluva pot of coffee, as I recall."

"He's out on the water," Maury said. "He said he'd catch a few fish for a fry tonight while Bonnie's beans are soaking. I've got to get back up to the front end." He spun and went across to the front door and went out it.

"I'll give Al a call as we head down to the water." Fergie handed the sheriff a mug that proclaimed, "I would agree with you, but then we'd both be wrong."

She led him down the stairs to the lower floor and out the door.

As they started down the first of the cement steps that led down to the water, he asked, "You want to tell me what's going on here?"

"I better let Al give you the scoop on that," Fergie said.

"Does he tell a better story than you?"

"Often, he does."

"Hmpf."

Fergie grinned to herself. Clayton had his white Stetson back on but he was down a few steps ahead of her, so she could see out across the water. A breeze tugged at her long red ponytail. Little tips of white showed on the cresting waves. A white bird flew low along the far shore, but she couldn't see Al's bass boat.

She took out her phone and speed-dialed him.

"Yeah?" he answered.

"Your ex-boss is here."

"What's he wearing?"

"Civvies."

"Uh-oh. How's he look?"

"You know, kinda tall and bulkish."

Al sighed. "I'll be right over."

In half a minute, she could see his boat coming their way from the left. "I knew he wouldn't be far. He had to be where he could keep an eye on this end of the property."

Clayton's head turned toward her, and his eyes narrowed in the shade beneath his hat's brim. "Maybe one of you can tell me what the hell's going on around here while I talk about my little issue."

Fergie just smiled. Al and Clayton had helped each other a few times after Al's retirement from the force, mostly Al doing favors for Clayton. But they were, first and foremost, friends. It tickled her a little, though, to see Clayton squirm a bit behind that stony mask his face usually was. Clayton finished what was left of the coffee in his mug and sprayed a bit of the last few remaining drops onto the grass. He handed the empty mug to Fergie.

Al slowed his boat and, with a practiced flair, turned off the motor and let it ease into the slip in the boat dock, a steel frame holding up a roof with an electric winch. He reached over and flipped a switch, and the two wide straps caught the weight of the boat and started up.

As soon as it was stable and just above the waterline, Al turned off the winch and hopped out to head their way.

"I think I have enough fish in the live well for our needs if Bonnie's got some cornbread going."

"She does," Fergie said.

"I've also got a whopping gar story. But I'll save that for later." As Al got close enough to shake Clayton's extended hand, he added, "If you're staying for dinner, I can go out and catch a couple dozen more fish."

"No need. I'll say my piece and be on my way." Clayton glanced at the boat, maybe wishing he was fishing more instead of running a populous county's sizeable sheriff's department. He turned back to Al. "Any reason you're carrying a sidearm and Maury's lugging a shotgun around at the end of your lane?"

Fergie waited to see how much Al would tell Clayton. So far, they hadn't asked for help from the department about trespassers, due in part to Al's experience as a former deputy. Ninety percent of the time, trespassing calls were just a nuisance.

"We had some nighttime visitors who got moved along."

"Did Annie Oakley Bonnie in there plug any of them?"

"Just a couple of harmless shots in the air. As she would say, it was as dark—"

"As the inside of a cow," Clayton finished for him. "Yet you're all still on the prod."

"They left behind a metal detector. Maury was messing around with it. A couple of guys came back and took it after knocking out Maury by holding him down and pinching his nose shut while holding a hand over his mouth."

"Doesn't he have a bad heart?"

"He's lucky to still be with us. He was roughed up some, and he's not very stout to begin with," Fergie said.

Clayton was watching Al's eyes as he kept a watch on the lake for any watercraft that might come their way. Two Jet Skis along the far shore looked like they were doing their best to ram each other amid a good deal of shouting and high sprays of water. But that was just the usual sort of knucklehead outdoor fun.

"Anyway, that's what we're up to at the moment." Al turned back to Clayton. "What's on your mind that brings you out here?"

"I've got a problem, one that could have political ramifications."

"You know I try to stay as far away as I can from politics," Al said.

"I'm aware of that. This also has a personal edge to it."

"The next election's barely a year away," Al said. "You've always won by a wide margin. I can take an educated guess at what you're going to say, but why don't you go ahead and say it."

"Someone, a woman, has made allegations of being abused by me, sexually."

"How long ago?" Fergie asked.

"She claims it happened thirty years ago."

"Good lord. That sort of thing makes no sense to me, and I'm a woman." Fergie shook her head hard enough to toss her red ponytail from side to side. "I know it was different times that long ago, but even if it was legitimate, to wait this long seems more whimsical than purposeful."

"And the claims are as hollow as Dan Bailey's wooden leg. Trust me."

"But the claim is there all the same."

"At first, it was just her. Then she rounded up another woman who came forward to say the same thing."

"Are they any part of your past?"

"I don't know them from Adam's house cat. Never heard of either one of them."

"Why do you think anyone would take them seriously?"

"Because today's media is hungry for anything with an edge, upsetting, or revolting. They grab and run with anything that feels like a story."

"Sounds to me like someone is after a defenestration," Fergie said. "Anything to get you out of office, however outrageous, if it just rocks the boat and sows seeds of doubt and distrust."

"Well, it's damn well trying to rock my boat. The thing about such accusations is that they can be as wispy and unfounded as you can imagine, but they cause damage. I personally think anyone making up such unfounded lies and getting caught out on it ought to be publicly spanked." Clayton's booming voice had risen to a near roar. Bonnie could probably hear him all the way up at the house.

"Barring that, what do you want from me?" Al's voice was much softer.

"I can't use my department. You know that. I was hoping you could freelance some poking about to disprove these allegations."

"I think you can see that we kind of have our hands full at the moment," Fergie said. "We believe whoever has been slipping onto the property will do so again. They're not done yet, and what they want is unresolved. We have to be here and ready."

"I could free up some men to swing by here, around the clock. That could take some pressure off you guys and your front end."

"I wouldn't know where to start." Al shook his head.

"I'll give you the names. You were a helluva detective, Al. Still are. All I want is for you to give me a hand. You're the only one I can count on for this."

Fergie had never before seen such a hangdog look on Clayton's face. She knew right then that Al would crumble and help.

Chapter Seven

The sun dimmed and brightened again as clouds slid over the sun outside the tightly closed venetian blinds. The motel room grew darker and lighter accordingly, with only the reading light behind Budge and his book lighting the room.

Griff lay sprawled on one of the two twin beds, staring up at the swaying cobwebs in one corner of the room. "Why don't you slip down to the corner and pick us up a pizza? We have just about enough left for that."

"Why not get it delivered?"

"Costs more, and then there's the tip."

"I'm reading."

"And I'm thinking hard about some kind of diversion that could get us safely back on that property. Which is likely to pay more?"

"Okay, then." Budge put the empty envelope in the book as a bookmark and closed it. He rose slowly and lumbered toward the motel room door.

Griff continued to stare, barely hearing the snick as the door closed. He wasn't coming up with much. Sometimes in the past, if he just gave himself time, an opportunity or suggestion would tumble into his path, like that time someone's wallet just happened to come into his hands that had the person's ATM PIN written on a piece of paper. That had been the windfall he needed and had got them by for a spell. But like all good things, it came to an end when the guy called the bank to shut down the mini Niagara of money flow for Griff.

Forty minutes later, a knock sounded at the door.

"Come in. You've got a key."

Nothing.

So Griff pried himself loose from the bed and went over to open the door, only to realize he should have looked through the peephole first.

There stood Moog Palance, in a dark suit with almost invisible pinstripes, as well as with a glitter in his eyes so full of hate and scorn that they made him look like a cross-eyed snake. His probably dyed hair was pale blond and frizzled out in a cross between Einstein and Bob Dylan. But that in no way made him look warm and fuzzy. Behind him stood two of his much taller goons, who looked like gym rat UFC wannabees. They had probably spent time in front of mirrors practicing how to make their faces look menacing.

Moog was about five feet four or so. Griff had known him since high school when he was known as "Li'l" Moog until bad things started happening to those who called him that. Most notably, the marching band's drum major got pushed down a set of stairs and ended up with a broken leg just prior to the homecoming game. The drum major had not been inclined to explain how it had happened, and he steered widely clear of Moog ever after that.

"I'm here for the vig, Griff, on the five large you borrowed from me."

"How'd you find me?"

"I have people for that sort of thing. Besides, you're a little rat, and you'd be down one rathole or another."

"I don't have it. I told you I'm working on something. I'll pay you. But I'm tapped at the moment."

Moog's eyes lowered and fixed on the glitter on Griff's wrist. "You're dressin' pretty fine. Did you spend the dough on threads? And is that thing on your arm real?"

Griff nearly said he thought Moog dressed fairly well himself and not nearly so much like something out of a would-be mobster's handbook as he might have expected. But he saw nothing to joke about on the grim, frowning faces of the two men hovering behind Moog. Their suits looked like they'd come off the rack at JCPenney, but the suit jackets had plenty of room to hide shoulder holsters.

Suddenly, their heads went together with a crack. One slumped to the ground. The other tried to turn in slow motion, but a giant fist hammered down on his head. He fell to the walkway outside the door as well. Then Budge stood where they had been, and he was grinning.

As Moog spun to have a look, his hand went inside his jacket, but Budge's hand was quicker and came out holding the gun Moog was going for, a pearl-handled Colt .25 automatic, a small person's gun, not good for much except shooting someone close in the belly.

Budge popped out the clip and jacked the shell out of the chamber and tossed everything onto the nearest bed.

"You'll get your money, Moog. Just give us time," Griff said. "We're good for it. In the meantime…"

Budge had already slipped his book into a small brown canvas duffel bag. As he went back out the door, he stepped over the two men sprawled across the walkway to stand, holding the door for Griff, who only had to scrape his shaving things into a small hard-shell suitcase. He grabbed a hanging garment bag and shot out the door. Griff also had to step over and around the two guys crumpled on the walkway outside the door. As he started to clatter down the metal stairs to the parking lot, he expected Moog to be going for his gun. But the little guy stood in the doorway, talking into his phone. He didn't have time to speculate about who Moog was calling. All he knew was they had to move like lightning, which would be something of a feat, given his vehicle.

"JUST FOLLOW THEM, AND don't lose them. Don't let them see you on their tail either. I want to know what he's up to." Moog put his phone away and went to get his small pistol off the bed and reload it.

On the walkway outside the door, one of his downed men began to stir.

Moog went over and nudged the guy with the toe of his wing tip shoe. "C'mon, you guys. Snap to. We got work to do."

Chapter Eight

Fenster sat behind the wheel of Moog's battleship-gray Lincoln Town Car. He saw a battered red Ford 150 pull into one of the motel's parking spaces. A big fellow, more muscle than fat and wearing jeans and a red T-shirt, got out while carrying a pizza box. He started to go up the metal stairs to the next floor.

In just a few moments, back down the stairs came the guy with the pizza box in one hand and a small duffel in the other. Another fellow, far more nicely dressed, came scampering down the stairs right behind him, carrying another small suitcase and garment bag.

Fenster's phone rang. It was Moog.

"Stay with the car," Moog ordered, so he did.

He waited until the red truck had gone briskly to the motel exit and shot out onto the street before he turned on his engine. For three years, he'd driven a getaway car for two friends who were now cooling their heels behind bars, so he didn't doubt he could catch up to the truck and keep it in sight.

The gas tank was almost full, and the big car glided in and out of traffic, keeping far enough back and moving about enough not to be a steady presence in a rearview mirror. The guys in the truck didn't seem to tumble to Fenster, but every once in a while, he'd pull over or hang back to disappear altogether, then he'd rush to catch up.

Once, he thought he might have lost them but then saw them going down a ramp to a service station with a convenience store. He took the next exit, did a U-turn in the turnabout, and headed back along the access road until he could cross over and pull into the station to slip into the far back of the lot by the air pump.

Fenster cracked his windows and turned off the engine, the AC with it. A warm wind swept in through the top of the windows. It would soon be up to a hundred degrees. He would in a short while have a patina of sweat on his brow, but he didn't turn the air back on.

He could see the truck from where he sat. His phone rang.

It was Moog asking, "Anything going on?"

"They're sitting in their truck, eating pizza after getting a couple of those big seventy-two-ounce soft drinks each."

"They're low on cash, I'm guessing. Not enough for vig, and they'd already checked out of that flop of a motel. Any idea what they'll do next?"

"Not unless you count taking a really big pee at some point in their future."

"Well, keep after them... and keep me informed."

As he put the phone down, the big guy smashed the pizza box and jammed it into a trash can. The minute he was back in the truck, it started to pull out of where it was parked.

"WHY'D YOU HAVE TO BORROW the money from someone like Moog Palance? You know he's just a little bit crazy." Budge was looking steadily ahead when Griff glanced his way.

Griff also gave the rearview mirror an occasional peek but mainly focused on driving steadily while thinking ahead to where they might possibly crash and what they were going to use for money to do so. "I've known Moog from way back. He was easy to touch, and who knew he was going to get so pissy about five large?"

"Let's just get our hands on that gold before the vig gets so big you can never pay it."

"It does tend to do that." He didn't look at Budge. "What're you going to get when we get our hands on all that gold?"

"I'm gonna buy books and read all day long and never work again."

"You know, there's this thing called a library card. You could get one and read books for free. Ever think of that?"

Budge tilted his head. "Well, what do you care? You're probably gonna give most of yours to your floozy."

"She likes to be called by her stage name, Tyrza Floen, and she does have dollar signs in her eyes. But let me tell you, she's worth it, worth it all."

"I guess I'm not keen on the idea of payin' for it."

"You know I could get all I want for free. I visited the Virgin Islands once, and after that, they were just called the Islands."

"I think I heard or read that somewhere before."

Griff drove, passing a wide field that sloped up to a ridge of rocks. On the other side of a neighboring fence, a herd of longhorns grazed, but the field he was looking at was a stretch of blackened land. A fire had swept through, and where it had come across the open range, thick stands of prickly pear cactus looked like twisted chunks of licorice. The rains had stopped falling not long before, and the lake levels would soon be dropping. Grasses were turning yellow, and when some tomfool tossed a cigarette out the window of a car, a fire started with leaping yellow tongues. Even stopping over dry patches of grass on the shoulders would let the catalytic converter of a vehicle act like a torch on the ready tinder of dry grass below.

He'd seen the blackened field before, and though he thought he'd been rambling about on the roads to give himself time to think, he knew where he was headed, where they *had* to go. They had no place to stay and no money. They had to take the risk and get back on the property where the stagecoach station had stood.

"Are we...?"

"Yeah, Budge. We gotta try unless you've got a better idea."

Budge was silent for a mile or so. "Well, I guess if we check first and are really, really careful."

"That's right. They probably won't even be on their toes, and no one else knows where we are at all."

FERGIE CAME OUT OF the master bedroom, wearing a red evening gown that swept down to midcalf but also dipped at the top to a hint of cleavage.

Bonnie looked up from where she was loading dishes into the dishwasher. "Yowza. Yowza. You going full-scale Mata Hari on this guy?"

"It just happened that I know the editor who is sitting on the story."

"When you say 'know,' do you mean in the biblical sense? Like he lay with her and knew her well?"

"We were friends."

"You're not dressed like a friend."

"Okay. We dated. That was long ago. Where we're meeting to chat requires a little panache."

"How'd you find out he was the one with the story?"

"He called Clayton, wanted to give him a chance to tell his side of the story. Clayton, of course, said there was no side to his story. When, thirty years after the fact, a couple of women spring up out of nowhere with anything like a sexual abuse charge, you have to doubt it. But the allegations alone could do serious damage, especially as close as this to a coming election year for the sheriff."

"Al didn't want to meet this editor and rattle the information out of him?"

"The truth is neither of us have had as much experience with this sort of thing. We barely know where to start. The names of the two alleged victims would be a good place, and I was best suited to go after that. It's bad enough we have to bother with this just now, when we're forced to keep a thorough and careful eye on the property, but Clayton asked the favor, and that's how it works."

Bonnie shook her head at Fergie's stunning outfit again. "Are you sure a black leather outfit and a whip might not work better with this guy you're meeting?"

"Probably not. This guy might bruise like a grape."

EVENING WAS SETTLING in, and the sky was dimming, but the heat wasn't letting up. Griff had his arm out the open driver's-side window. He slowed the truck as they passed the lane going back to the former stagecoach station property. The smells of hot asphalt and drying vegetation rose up to him.

From the other direction, a sheriff's department SUV cruiser came their way, the deputy inside glancing toward the same property that interested Griff. "Not a good sign," he muttered to Budge.

"Are you sure about this?" Budge asked.

"You got any better ideas about someplace where we might stay for free and think hard about what to do, or are we just gonna do it?"

Budge didn't respond but looked out his window, and Griff went back and forth looking into each property along the way. The houses weren't jammed right up against each other out that way, and a lot of trees, bushes, and other vegetation insulated the abodes from each other.

The sky had dimmed to near black before Griff tentatively turned into one drive and eased back into what turned out to be an empty lot. He thought it had looked that way, which made it nearly perfect if they didn't have to go through or around a couple of other lots with houses.

Griff got out of the truck and took a quick look around to ensure that it was empty and that he could see neither of the neighboring houses from where he was parked. He looked down at the lane, and his tracks were the only ones that had come in for a while. He got a flashlight out of the glove box he'd bought earlier, complete with fresh batteries for their last mini exploration of the property. Budge hauled out the metal detector, which he held in one hand, his hand lantern in the other. Griff locked the truck and started up the lane toward the road, having decided going across other people's properties was too risky.

The grass had yellowed and bent along the sides of the lane. When they stepped on it, the sound was like the crunch of stepping on Rice Krispies. The heat was oppressive, still over a hundred even that late in the evening. He was soon sweating through his shirt. Budge was huffing as he walked beside Griff, and he seemed to ooze a cautious tension, taking each step with care and looking around constantly.

Near the road, they turned off their lights, looked both ways, then eased out onto the road. As they walked in the direction of the place, Griff kept his eye on the wooded areas around them, planning ahead on where they could dash if they had to get off the road when a car or truck came along it.

"Feeling better about this?" Griff asked.

"Nope."

They trudged up the road, not speaking, listening hard to the rustle of leaves in the treetops and on the forest floor around them, all as dry as could be.

FENSTER RANG UP MOOG on the phone.

"Yeah? What is it?" Moog answered.

"I think you might want to send your guys Ike and Rueben out this way. Our pair of songbirds are making their move, and they've got a metal detector. That's where some of your five g's went."

"What the hell are they gonna do with that? And where the hell are you?"

"I don't know what they're planning, but if it's about money, I thought you'd like to know. As for where I am, I'm not entirely sure myself. Out by Lake Travis's shoreline in some bumfart nowhere corner. But I'll guide the guys this way if you get them headed out here."

"Got it. Just so you know, one of them might be a little wonko. I'd guess he has a concussion."

"How'd that happen?"

"The big one. I'd stay clear of him if you can."

"Words to the wise. I'll do it. Now, are they coming out here?"

"Consider them mobilized." The phone clicked off.

Chapter Nine

Bonnie walked out to the end of the lane until she could see the road just ahead. She had the 30-06 over her shoulder on its strap. The clip was full, and she had an extra box of ammo in her pocket. She stood still and gave a low whistle.

A rustle from her right began and grew until Maury came pushing his way through the crackling, drying brush, making a little more noise than a herd of buffalo. Her pappy had drilled into her how to be as quiet as a mouse stealing cheese while going through the woods, even one getting as brittle and snappy as the one around the house had become.

"I'm glad to see you," Maury said. "I was getting a mite peckish."

"Well, get a move on. Tanner's the only one watching over Little Al, although he was asleep when I come out here. Don't get into those beans, though. They're only soaking and won't be fit to eat until I've cooked them tomorrow."

"I've seen sheriff's department cruisers going by on the road every now and again. That's comforting to know." He stood straighter and reached to hold his back. "I needed a break anyway. I'm starting to feel my age."

"I know. I've heard your creaks and moans. But I know something that will make you feel younger."

"Indeed you do. Maybe we can wrangle some 'us' time again soon."

"You bet." She grinned at him. "It'll happen."

He started to walk back to the house but stopped. He turned to look at her. "I've been foolish and selfish."

"How so?"

"I did the math. I'm going to be far from young when Little Al graduates from high school. Will I even be around to guide and care for him?"

"Sure you will," Bonnie said. "You're just as young as you feel... or the person you feel, and that's me."

"You do keep me feeling spry."

THE TWO OF THEM HAD to duck off the road a half dozen times during their hike toward the lane of the property they sought. When they came to it, Griff kept going.

Budge reached to tap his shoulder. "Aren't we going onto the property?"

"Yeah, but not right down the lane to the house. I figure if we come in from the other side, that would be least expected. It'll also give us a chance to take a better look at those horseshoes and wheel rims. I'm pretty sure this is where the old stagecoach station sat, but it won't hurt to cross our *t*'s and dot our *i*'s."

Budge shrugged and trudged along beside him, ready at any second to dart off the paved two-way road again.

A PAIR OF HEADLIGHTS pulled up slowly behind the car where Fenster sat waiting. The lights went out, and the doors on each side opened.

He watched his rearview mirror until he was sure Ike and Rueben were the ones getting out of the vehicle. They'd followed his instructions to get to the spot, but he wanted to make sure some deputy hadn't followed them.

As soon as they got to him and he could make out their faces, he could see Ike had a lump like half a tennis ball on the side of his head, and Rueben had a black eye that was nearly closed shut. The open eye seemed to wander somewhat, perhaps because of a concussion. Not the best warriors to send into a fray, but they were dealing with amateurs here, he figured.

"Where's the big one?" Ike held what looked like an Uzi toward Fenster, not his first pick of a submachine gun. Rueben held a .357 Ruger with a six-inch matted rib barrel down at his side. That was a good gun but old enough the bluing had been worn down to the steel in places.

"They both headed up the road a ways toward the target property."

"What's up there?" Rueben reached to touch what must have been a rather sore eye. "What're they up to?"

"I have no idea. I think Moog wants you to follow them and figure out what this is about. No need to engage them."

"Oh, I don't know." Ike shook his head. "I get anywheres near that guy again, I'm a gonna have to open a can of whoop-ass on him."

"Well, you'd better get going... and take it easy. Remember, there might be money in this somewhere, and you both know how Moog feels about money."

A PICKUP TRUCK WAS coming, so Griff led the way in a quick scamper off the road into a dying stand of sumac that surrounded the base of a huge pecan tree.

Budge crowded close beside him as the truck with its hideously bad muffler thundered past.

As soon as it was by them, Griff whispered, "Now we backtrack into the property. No lights."

"Why're you whispering?" Budge asked.

"We were shot at the last time we were here. This is not the kind of place where we can expect warm embraces. So shush."

Even moving as silently as they could, going soundless was a challenge with the crisp dried leaves and grass on the ground in the woods. Small broken twigs gave crisp snaps as well. Twice, Griff stopped and held up a hand, trying to get Budge to move more silently.

They could hear dry leaves rustling in the treetops and the occasional scamper of something small moving swiftly away. The sliver of moon showed through the treetops just enough for them to barely see where they were going.

BONNIE'S EARS WERE perked, and her eyes squinted in alertness. She'd hunted many a night like that with her pappy, enough to know to sit still and let moving things come toward her. For a few minutes, she'd been listening to a steady rustle and crackle off in one direction. That was no coon or possum. Those were big feet crushing, crackling, and snapping. She'd gone into extreme stealth mode and already had a shell jacking into the rifle's chamber. Using the scope, she was peering through the dim trunks of trees as she swept the gun's barrel back and forth across the area where she heard the sounds coming from. Somebody had no more woods smarts than some greenhorn city slicker.

Then she could make out two forms pushing through some waist-high stickery chaparral she would surely have avoided. They were floundering, not seeing well at all. But one of them suddenly raised a pistol at a sound he'd heard, probably an owl.

Bonnie settled the crosshairs on the man's left buttock and slowly squeezed the trigger.

Bam!

A scream split the night, and the two spun and started off in the other direction, one limping like the dickens.

She had a bead on the other one but would have hit him squarely in the back. But she didn't want to kill them just yet. Maybe a good scare would do the trick.

Bonnie chuckled. *There's nothing like taking a bullet to the keister to say, "You're not welcome!"*

FENSTER STOOD OUTSIDE the car and was leaning against it when he heard the exaggerated rustle of leaves, dry grass, and twigs snapping and crackling like two bulls were coming through the woods.

He'd heard the siren and seen the lights of a sheriff's department cruiser racing by out on the road, so he had a hunch about how Moog's thugs had done.

Ike and Rueben came bursting out of the vegetation. Rueben was limping, and Ike had an arm around him, helping him. Fenster could see blood on Rueben's pant leg. He'd lost his pistol somewhere along the way.

"Give me a hand," Rueben said. "Someone's gone and shot me in the ass. Lucky they weren't a good shot."

"Don't kid yourself. That was on purpose," Fenster said.

"That's right," Ike agreed. "You coulda been killed."

"Did you see those other two out there?" Fenster asked.

"Nope. All we saw was someone shooting at us."

"And not missing," Rueben said, reaching back with one hand to his rear. "Shot me right in the butt. Coulda killed me."

"I have a hunch that if that shooter wanted to kill you, you'd still be laying back there," Fenster said.

"Why would anyone *want* to go on that property? I'd sooner make a try on Fort Knox." Ike shook his head.

"That's what they want you to think. But if those other two can get onto the place, we can," Rueben said.

"Sure. Given the splendid job you've done so far." Fenster opened the driver's-side door to the Town Car.

"Give me a ride to a doc," Rueben said.

"You're not going to bleed all over the seats of this car," Fenster said. "And don't go to a hospital with a bullet wound. Go to Moog. He'll know some freelancing sawbones who can tend to you. You'd best get moving. You're still bleeding, you know."

"If I die on the way back to town, I'm never gonna forgive y'all," Rueben said.

Fenster shook his head, got into his car, and started the motor. He waited until the other two headed out onto the road before he eased out, looked both ways, and headed back to town himself. He reached for his phone. He needed to let Moog know what to expect, and he didn't imagine he was going to be very happy.

Chapter Ten

The back streets of the Clarksville section of Austin were dimly lit beneath a black sky as Fergie found a place to park at last. She looked around as she got out of her car but saw no one lurking about. For a second or two, she thought about the house by the lake and her family, but nothing much was likely to happen that night. So she started off down Lynn Street toward Jeffrey's, a neighborhood-looking cozy little restaurant that disguised one of the finer dining spots in all the city, though it was too embedded in the little cottage homes of the area to have valet service.

She and Klive Henning had gone there many times when dating, but she kept her eyes open, all too aware that she held only a tiny clutch purse and her Glock was in the glove box of the car. She saw only one or two people on the street and heard a dog barking insistently in the distance.

She came to the striped awnings and slipped inside the front door. She always felt like she was entering someone's home.

At the far back corner table on the left, their usual spot, Klive stood up from the table, all six feet five of him, and she headed his way.

He winked at her outfit. "Charmed," he said as he helped her into her seat. He still had his British accent and wore, of all things, a brown tweed jacket despite the heat of the day outside, which was only beginning to fade as the evening settled in.

The amber glow of the soft lighting showed enough of Klive's clean-shaven face to confirm that he was aging in a quite normal and graceful way. They were the same age, and it had been a relief to her back then to be able to look up at the face of her date. She had also always enjoyed his urbane old-world manners.

"Let me guess," she said. "You have your heart set on the lamb."

"I've already ordered it, and fish for you. The halibut's been just flown in, fresh as it can be."

Soft music and the hum of others talking masked the silent steps of the waiter placing an hors d'oeuvres plate of warm olives and toasted nuts onto the table then filling her glass from a bottle of 2018 Ducru-Beaucaillou Saint-Julien French Bordeaux, "Le Petit Ducru." Everything reminded her of why they had come to the place so often, pricey as it was.

Fergie took a sip of her wine, looking over the rim of the glass at Klive, whose large brown eyes always seem to brim with compassion and a sparkle of curiosity.

"Would you like to cut to the chase before we dine or have it as a dessert?"

"'If it were done when 'tis done, then 'twere well it were done quickly,'" she said.

"Ah, you haven't forgotten my love of the Bard. How we could all use a Lady Macbeth around some days." He took a small sip of his wine. "I suppose Clayton sent you."

"In a manner. He *is* concerned."

"He should be. This isn't the sort of thing I would normally publish in *The Probe*."

"That's a lie. It's exactly the sort of article you'd gobble up and publish as long as you had thoroughly checked your facts and sources."

"Okay. You have me there. What did Clayton tell you? He rather told me to buzz off. His words."

"He said he has no memory of the event and categorically denies the whole thing."

"But it could still hurt him, possibly cost him the next election."

"There's that. But it doesn't even sound like him. He was married at the time."

"Yet the two ladies, who were both seventeen at the time, made statements that Clayton was a deputy who came to speak at their Girl Scout jamboree, and he stayed the night in one of the cabins. The sex, they say, was consensual—they admit to slipping into his cabin—but they were nevertheless underage, which also means that there is no statute of limitations on a statutory rape charge."

The waiter appeared soundlessly beside their table and slipped their entrées in front of them. The fish did look divine, the oven-roasted Washington halibut surrounded by short rib ravioli, roasted root vegetables, red grapes, and parsley. His lamb osso buco looked pretty good too. It was like old times for them.

"You know what I'm going to ask you." Fergie broke off a piece of fish with her fork and swept it through the sauce.

"You know that would be trading on a favor, which is borderline blackmail, don't you know."

"Borderline? It's crossed the border and is coming back with Mexican takeout," she said. "You know you owe me big."

He sighed. "So it's come to this."

They had been close friends for a long time, so it pained her to put the vise grips to him. But she had a deeper loyalty to Al, and he to Clayton. The thing was that though she and Klive had dated for some time, years before, the physical side had never gone beyond a kiss on the cheek as he dropped her off at her door. That had told her a lot.

In those days, it wasn't uncommon for a man to be deeply in the closet about his preferences. He had never said a thing about any of that, but it hadn't taken her long to realize their platonic friendship was a "beard" of sorts to make him show well in public. He was a great conversationalist, and she couldn't have asked for a more polite and caring companion. She hated to use what she knew for leverage, and even then, she felt no reason to talk openly about any of that.

He reached into his inside jacket pocket and brought out a couple of folded papers. "It's all there: names, addresses, and the date in July thirty years ago. I was going to identify the two women by the pseudonyms Jen and Sam. Just do me one favor, if you will be so kind."

"Done," she said. "If I uncover anything that drives a spike in this particular cannon, I'll let you know right away so you don't paint yourself into some political and legal corner."

"Thanks ever so much. Now let's just enjoy this fine meal and each other."

She finished putting the papers into her clutch without looking at them. She looked across the table at him, his mouth twisted into a slightly ironic grin. "Fine, let's do just that."

On her way home, after taking a quick peek at the names and addresses of the two accusers, she played back the part of the conversation that hadn't happened. She could have said, "Say hello to Jabob for me."

His eyes would have opened wider, and he would have asked, "You know his name?"

"I'm a detective," she might have said.

But that might have been hurtful, and she saw no need for it among close platonic friends. Plus, she knew she had a scab or two he might have picked at. They'd known each other for quite a long time. To her, one of the most important aspects of life was to have friends who truly valued each other's company, conversation, and understanding. She would not ever wish to put a damper on something as noble and worthy as that.

She felt a twinge at having to pressure the bit of information she needed out of Klive, but he had come prepared to give it. They understood each other that well.

Chapter Eleven

When Fergie turned into the lane, her headlights swept across a sheriff's department SUV cruiser parked to one side, the dome light on with a deputy sitting inside.

"Uh-oh," she said to herself. Something had happened while she was away.

The deputy waved to her as she eased past the cruiser, heading back to the house.

Most of the lights were on, so everyone was up. She locked her car and went to the front door. As soon as she stepped inside, she asked, "Who did Bonnie shoot this time?"

Tanner got up from where he'd been curled up near Al's feet. He, Bonnie, and Maury were sitting around the dining table, drinking coffee, late as it was. Al got up and came toward her.

"Nobody got hurt?" Fergie asked. Al put his arms around her.

"Not on our side," Bonnie said, "but one o' them is sporting a sore dairy air."

"Is no one watching the back end, down by the lake?" Fergie hugged Al back with a little touch of extra enthusiasm.

"In addition to a cruiser parked up front, Clayton has a department boat giving that end of the property a sweep every now and then. He said it's the least he could do since we're helping him with his issue. He wants us to get one good night of sleep so we'll be fresh and rested. We are making progress, aren't we?"

"Small steps at first. But I have names and addresses now, a starting point." Fergie fished the paper Klive had given her out of her clutch. She opened it. "The two seventeen-year-old girls, thirty years ago, were

Kristina Smeerna and Jacqueline Frineman. Klive made a note that the second one is sometimes known as Wacky Jacky. She was the instigator of what they say was consensual but, of course, still illegal."

"Girl Scouts," Maury said. "Was there a merit badge for dalliance back then?"

"Catch me up on what happened here at the house." Fergie put the paper down on the table and looked at each of them, stopping at Bonnie.

"Not a big deal," Bonnie said. "I was on patrol at the front end and spotted a couple of guys comin' through the rye. I popped one of them where it won't be fun sitting, and they took off like scalded cats."

"Probably won't do any good to call the hospitals and see if anyone showed up with a bullet wound," Fergie said.

"They'd have to be smarter than that, though they did come back onto the property after being shot at before. So they have some deep and dark reason, though I'm hard pressed to know what it is." Al shook his head.

"What's our plan for the morning?" Fergie asked.

"Maybe you can talk to one or both of these ladies."

"If I can. At the least, I could do a stakeout and see if they lead me anywhere."

"We couldn't spare you for long. We're going to have to step up our security around here."

"I could do one of the stakeouts," Maury said, "if you all can spare me here."

"That would be a help. Right now, we don't know where they work, what their usual routine is, and especially what motivated them to make their accusations now, suddenly, after thirty years." Al picked up the paper with the names and addresses and handed it to Maury. "Even if this really happened, which I'm prone to doubt, knowing Clayton, this whole thing smells of bad cabbage this close to a coming election."

"I say we all get to bed and grab some shut-eye," Bonnie said, "since that's what Clayton is giving us for the night."

They all headed for their bedrooms, Maury with a glitter in his eyes since Bonnie could be pretty peppy right after she shot someone. It seemed to stoke her libido, and that, of course, did the job for his.

Chapter Twelve

Moog sat in the back corner inside a Starbucks. Only those willing to brave the heat of a morning already warming up to a toastlike quality sat outside. Fenster went over to the small white table and sat across from him.

"Did you hear from your guys, Ike and Rueben?" he asked.

"Yeah, they went to see Doc Samuels. He was able to patch Rueben's butt. I didn't let either of them know he's a dentist. Malpractice is malpractice, and he's glad to get any business at all tossed his way these days."

"That would've been a helluva wound to explain at any hospital's ER."

"Did you do like I asked and see what you could find out about that property and why it might interest the likes of Griff and Budge?"

"Yeah, I did. But it's a bit of a head-scratcher."

"Try me."

"The property's owned by a guy who's a retired detective from the sheriff's department. He recently married a woman who is a retired city cop detective."

"I like it when old folks feel the sparks of new romance at that age. And that answers one puzzle about where Griff or Budge might've suddenly gotten their hands on a gun."

"It doesn't tell us what became of them."

"You think they got nabbed for trespassing?"

"Nope. Their raggedy-ass truck was gone from where they thought they'd secretly parked it."

"Now to the more important question," Moog said. "Where's the money?"

"Damned if I know. They have older vehicles, and he has an eight-year-old bass boat. No conspicuous expenditures I could find out at all. It is a lakefront property, but I don't know how that ties to anything, especially something that calls for a metal detector."

"That part's your key. Keep digging. See what you can find out. It would help if you could lay hands on that Griff or his lumpy sidekick. They must have an idea about it."

"Hard to tell where they are right now. Their blip has sure sailed off the radar for now."

GRIFF'S EYES SNAPPED open. He was looking up at fragments of dawn-tinted sky through the thick leaves of a canopy formed by three huge pecan trees embracing each other's limbs. A breeze rustled the leaves, a breeze that felt cool to him though the morning was probably eighty degrees and on its way to one hundred again. He wore only his boxer shorts and socks.

He had hung his clothes neatly on a hanger from his garment bag on a board jutting from the partially collapsed red barn just a few feet from them, past the big trees. They were old pecans, already big when the Comanche and Kiowa tribes rode rampant through the area.

He sat up and looked around, rubbing at his back where he had lain against the ridges that lined the bottom of the truck bed. Before he fell asleep, despite the heat, he had seen stars and watched clouds hiding and revealing the moon through the swaying tops of the trees.

The door to the truck's cab opened, and Budge climbed out and stretched. He'd kept his clothes on, and even with the windows cracked, his red T-shirt was soaked with sweat. It had to have been hot as an oven in there. He tugged at the shirt plastered to him. "I believe it was General Sherman who said that if he owned Texas and hell, he'd rent out Texas and live in hell."

"He'd have gotten my vote on that," Griff agreed.

"We sure made tracks outta there last night when we heard a gunshot."

"Leaving was the right thing to do at that moment, but it leaves us with a problem."

"Figuring who was shooting and at what?"

"I'm just glad it wasn't us." Griff went over to his clothes, took down the pants, and dressed as he spoke. Of the two of them, he had to maintain a level of panache and style and to do so with élan. He knew that, with all his reading, Budge was probably smarter than he was. Curiosity and the drive to devour books made Budge more informed. But his size and accidental brutality was another whole dimension. Griff's wheelhouse was being glib, ready with an excuse or a quick way out of a mess. He would have to be the one to come up with something clever in the moment.

"Our problem is we have no money," he said, "no place to stay, and no way to feed ourselves."

"I am hungry."

"Welcome to the club."

"We could get jobs."

"And get paid in a week? We'd darn near starve first. No, we've got to take action."

"But..."

"We can't live like this. We've gotta take some risks, and soon."

"You mean rob some convenience store or something?"

"That's not our style either, and I'm opposed to jail or prison time."

He slowly finished dressing, feeling more dapper. He looked around. They were on a property he'd spotted along Nameless Road that had a For Sale sign by the open gate. Providing no overzealous real estate agent wanted to show the property, which wasn't all that much to look at, a burned-out farmhouse and a collapsed barn, they could stay where they were until dark.

"We need a distraction."

"A fire?"

"No. We need the woods around that house the way it is if we're to get any sneaking about done at all. A fire would make the property too open."

"If flames took the house and maybe the people in it, we could look around better."

"Really? You're up to murder? You only accidentally killed a guy once. Plus, if they've got a dog, you'd be sicker about hurting it than the people."

"I did think I heard a bark or two. So, yeah, they probably have a dog."

"Which also doesn't help our chances of sneaking onto the place."

"I suppose a tunnel is out of the question."

"Do you want to dig it? With no food in us?"

"No."

"We can hardly go to Moog and ask for more money."

"He's sure some kind of Loan Stranger, isn't he? I mean *l-o-a-n*."

Griff didn't laugh at Budge's attempt to be funny. "He's almost certainly in a foul mood at the moment. I wouldn't want to be seen by him or his men just now."

"What're we going to do today?" Budge asked. "I mean besides not eating."

"Let's pool our money, see if we have enough for coffee and a doughnut each."

"I don't have any money left. How about you?"

"Nope, and any credit cards I had are tapped out and turned off. So we have squat. It looks like a long, hungry day waiting on it to get dark."

"Then what?"

"We'll go take a close look at that property again. Maybe an opportunity will present itself."

"There's one thing that puzzles me quite a bit." Budge scratched at his head.

"What's that?"

"A shot was fired, but not at us. Who was that bullet meant for?"

"You've got me. There's a lot about this that's puzzling me more than it should." Griff shook his head.

"Well, I can always read." Budge reached into the truck and pulled a book out of his bag. "At least this should keep me from thinking about food." He opened the tailgate, sat on it, and opened the book.

"Sure am hungry, though," Griff said.

Budge's big head rose, and his eyes tightened into a squint. "I said we're *not* gonna think about food." The words had an edge and came out as a threat.

Griff closed his mouth and kept it that way as he fussed with his clothes. He rarely admitted it to himself, but he was a little wary and fearful around Budge at times. Sure, they had been best buds for a long time, but there was more than a little sound of a ticking bomb about Budge. The guy had killed a man and had tied up another in bad weather for mistreating a dog. So it was going to be a long day without food and without talking.

FENSTER SAT ACROSS the desk from Moog, who felt a desk gave him more of a look of running things. Moog had been frowning to himself when Fenster came into the room, with its mostly empty bookshelves and a window that looked out across the parking lot behind the building.

"I want you to have Ike and Rueben stake out that property. Watch for Griff and Budge."

"Seems like a lot of effort for five g's."

"I don't want word to get out that anyone can get by with stiffing me."

"Rueben's hardly in shape to be out and about, watching some property."

"Get him a chair."

"He might not be ready for sitting a lot."

"Get him one of them round blow-up cushions. He'll work if he wants to stay on the payroll. And round him up another Ruger .357 like the one he left behind in his last dash off that property. I'll take what you have to pay for it out of his salary."

"Will do."

Chapter Thirteen

As the sun came up, Fergie was already in position, sitting in her car half a block away from the front doors of the Branching Arms condo complex in South Austin, not far from Zilker Park. Even at that hour, the drive into town had been a royal pain as commuters poured into the city, once peaceful but more recently a bustling metropolis growing ever outward into an urban sprawl that was beginning to reach all the way out to Al's home. People could buy property and homes for far less and were willing to commute to their jobs.

On top of having to maneuver her way through a sea of self-absorbed drivers, a third of them more interested in their cell phones than in fellow motorists, she hated to leave the house short-handed on the constant watch they all shared. Plus, the sun had been beaming straight into her eyes the whole way in. But they had promised to help Clayton, who had done them many a favor in the past.

She shrugged. She had done the battle getting to the building and had a good spot, so she reached for the thermos and the mug she'd brought. Steam rose from the coffee, and only a few people were stirring, coming out of the building, or getting into cars, some even close enough to their work to take off walking. Fergie had searched the internet and printed out photos of the two women. She almost thought "girls," which they had been once, and frisky ones if the version of that long-ago incident they'd shared with her friend Klive meant anything.

Fergie tried to think back to what she'd been doing at seventeen. Well, there was that disastrous prom date she'd had with Al. But she certainly hadn't been sneaking into any camp cabin in the middle of the night to have sex.

Kristina Smeerna and Jacqueline Frineman had lived lives totally different from hers.

Fergie had done a background check on them, and they were fairly clean if she discounted a few parking tickets and a speeding ticket by Jackie for doing forty-two in a thirty-five.

Roommates. Fergie could hardly imagine two high school chums living together for such a long time after their school days. She had to wonder too if they were sitting around one day and just said, "Hey, you know that thing that happened thirty years ago? Maybe we should do something about it." She wondered if the reason was social responsibility, or maybe it was about money. Many things were about money.

Fergie's credit check on them didn't show any problems or particularly good credit ratings. But they were hardly living high on the hog. Maybe that was the sort of glitter they were wanting in their lives.

Jacqueline Frineman, or Wacky Jacky, was the first to emerge from the building. Fergie had found photos of both women on the internet to help her identify them. She stayed on foot, not getting into a car, and headed down the street. Fergie slipped out of her car and stayed at a distance as she followed. Jacky had dyed red hair and a figure that was not winning its battle with gravity. Fergie had done the math, thirty years and seventeen. That made both women forty-seven, and they hadn't spent that time in a gym or married, from what Fergie could find out. Both still had their maiden names.

Jacky wore a white blouse with ruffles down the front that exaggerated her chest, a red plaid Catholic schoolgirl skirt that stopped mid-chubby-thigh, bobby sox, and what looked like sensible white sneakers. The overall effect seemed to be an effort to look young, which failed but prompted more pity than scorn.

Seven blocks from the condo, Jacky went into a diner that was brightly lit and already had a few coffee-and-doughnut types at the bar and a couple in a booth. She slipped on an apron and went around to check on the few customers. The stocky, balding guy back by the grill had probably taken care of the early firstcomers. Fergie supposed that the "Wacky Jacky" handle came from being the sort of waitress who had good days and bad. Heaven help the customer on her wacky days. Fergie had known a few servers like that.

Fergie made her way back to her car, slipped inside, and poured herself another mug of coffee as she continued her stakeout.

She waited nearly two hours for Kristina Smeerna to come down the steps. When she did, she glanced for a moment or two toward Fergie's car and seemed to spot her sitting in it. Then she headed the other direction but stayed on foot as well. She was more slender than Jacky and wore her hair blond although it was just as likely dyed. Fergie got out and had to tag along for nearly eleven blocks and one dogleg turn, with occasional glances back Fergie's way.

Kristina wore a black Kahot smock over a white blouse and tight jeans that showed off her sticklike legs. She also wore the sensible white sneakers of someone on their feet all day. She wore her hair in a ponytail that swayed back and forth as she walked. Her makeup was a tad over the top, with bright-red lips, thick blue eye shadow, and enough black mascara that when her eyes opened wide, they looked more fierce than frightened.

She suddenly spun and came striding back toward Fergie, who felt she needed to keep walking forward to seem natural.

Kristina's eyes narrowed, her nostrils flared, and most startling, her mouth showed her teeth in a threatening snarl, the opposite of a smile. "What's your deal? Are you following me? Why? What's the matter with you, anyway?"

"I think you're mistaken." Fergie sought an innocent and slightly outraged tone, but the blond woman wasn't having any of it. She was almost a head shorter than Fergie but wasn't backing down. In fact, she took a step closer and looked up at Fergie, who found it hard to believe that the other one was known as Wacky Jacky—this one looked ready to bite.

"Just get lost, see. I don't need some asshole like you in my day." She took on a little Edgar G. Robinson tone as she sought to sound tougher than she looked.

When Fergie just stood still, Kristina spun and marched off down the sidewalk. She didn't spit on the sidewalk, but that seemed to be her mood.

Barely half a block down the street, Kristina went into a hair salon. Fergie waited a while before she strolled casually by, and through the plate glass window, she saw Kristina inside, leading a customer to a chair and putting a hair-cutting apron on her across her chest and lap. She saw Fergie and, behind the customer's back, gave Fergie the finger.

So that was that. In moments, Fergie was back in her car, more puzzled than satisfied at what she'd accomplished. Maury had agreed to come back that evening and see what he could learn about the women, but Fergie didn't expect that to accomplish much.

As Fergie headed back to the house, she pondered the two women, who shared a nearly identical perpetual frown as they headed to work, both probably having lived on minimum wage for such a long time. That suggested they had neither the intelligence nor the ambition to do much else. *So what suddenly put a bee in their bonnets to dredge up their story about Clayton?* She mulled that over as she swept along in outward-bound traffic that was far easier to negotiate than the early-morning drive had been, although the sun was once again in her eyes.

GRIFF DIDN'T FEEL ANYWHERE close to his usual sartorial splendor when he had to leave his sport coat in its garment bag in the truck. His black mock turtleneck shirt was as good as a ninja outfit, while Budge wore a red T-shirt and jeans while carrying the metal detector.

The sky had been black when they started into the woods. He could barely see stars through the limbs above, and he hadn't seen anything of the moon yet. The ground was dry, and the vegetation crackled. The air smelled of dried dusty dirt and baked leaves. Whiffs of the grass had the odor of straw. They had no choice. They had to be out there. But after a day with no food or water, the night around them had the stink of doom and gloom—at least, it felt so to him.

Budge was once again making far more noise with his steps than Griff liked to hear. He stopped, and Budge bumped into him, stabbing him with the metal device he carried. Griff gave a start even though he knew Budge was right behind him. He glanced back and pointed in the direction where he'd seen some horseshoes and wagon wheel rims the older guy had uncovered.

His idea was to find that and start taking an outward spiral from there to find where the gold had been buried.

He stopped abruptly again and held a finger to his lips where Budge could see it. Griff had heard some rustling, then a step. Someone else was out in the woods at night.

AFTER GRABBING A QUICK bite of a beans-with-ham supper, with some of Bonnie's corn bread, of course, Fergie headed up the lane to take up watch near the road while Al kept a lookout from the shoreline. She had the 30-06's leather strap over her shoulder and a set of night vision goggles hanging at her neck since she had nowhere near the night eyes Bonnie did. Al had a myriad of useful gadgets in the bottom of the gun safe, and she had remembered the goggles just before heading out to her turn at the front end.

As she got closer to the road, the crispy dry trees and bushes around her suddenly seemed more somber, and she realized the woods was preternaturally quiet. As smoothly as she could, she slipped off to one side of the lane and stood for a moment beside the huge trunk of a live oak tree. In the still and dark of the night, she began to hear sounds, rustles, crunches, then more clearly, steps.

Fergie silently slid the night goggles on and scanned the woods ahead. She saw the big one first and heard him then realized a shorter man was ahead of him, his pale face beaming like a moon above his black shirt. The second one carried the metal detector that'd been on the property a short while, making these probably the ones who had roughed up Maury.

Just when she was about to slip off the goggles and switch to looking through the rifle's scope, she caught movement a ways behind the first two men. In a moment, Fergie could make out two more men, both carrying weapons. One of them was limping and wincing with each step.

Four men were too many for her to confront. She slid the goggles off to hang at her neck again. She took the rifle off her shoulder and raised it. Fergie peered through the scope, raised the crosshairs, above the second armed two, and squeezed off a shot that would go over their heads, but not by much. They might even hear the bullet whiz by.

Bam!

All hell broke loose.

The second two men swung their weapons toward her, one spraying bullets wildly with what sounded like an Uzi, a weapon she hadn't heard in a while but could readily recognize. She dropped to the ground right after letting off her own shot and could hear bullets clipping off twigs and causing dried leaves to sprinkle down all around her.

When she peeked around the bole of the tree with the goggles on again, she could see the front two men tearing through the woods, heading off to her right, while the two who had been behind them were steadily backing away while firing in her direction.

She lay still, giving them all time to make their getaways. A full fifteen minutes later, a sheriff's department cruiser came pulling into the lane with its lights and siren going.

"FASTER!" IKE YELLED back to Rueben.

"I'm going as fast as I can." He came limping along and made a sound with each step. "Ouch. Oh. Ow. Ouch. Umpf."

"Keep still back there."

"You try running with your ass half shot off."

By the time Rueben finally got to their car and tossed his Uzi in the back seat, Ike had the motor running, and they pulled out just after a cruiser went by, flashing blue and red lights, its siren going.

"Moog's gonna want to know what's going on back at that property," Ike said.

"I don't know what you're gonna tell him, because I have no earthly idea. I don't even think those guys we was following was the one who shot at us."

"Well, we'll talk it over with Moog. Maybe he's got some idea, 'cause I can't make any kind of sense outta this."

GRIFF WAS RUNNING AS flat out as he could go and right away was far behind the crashing, thrashing Budge. Big as he was, he was hurtling along like some Jamaican distance runner in the Olympics. The sound of gunfire will do that to those not accustomed to being in close proximity to it. At least this time, Budge was clinging to the metal detector like it was his child.

The thing about Texas is that nearly every plant has some thorn or sticker that wants to claw at anyone blindly running through the night, and Griff could feel the plants shredding his beloved corduroy slacks as well as doing his shirt a great deal of no good. But run he did as if it was for his life, and as far as he knew, it was.

MAURY GOT TO A PARKING spot where he could park Fergie's car close to the entrance of the Branching Arms condo complex before many of the residents got back from their jobs.

He got out of the car and took a short walk down to a park only a block square with a statue of someone in the middle, a frontiersman of some sort. From the size-twelve boots, he reckoned it could be Bigfoot Wallace. The sides of the park dipped down from the sidewalks, making it sort of a bowl shape, but that worked to the advantage of some small kids kicking around a soccer ball that would roll up one of the side slopes to come right back down toward them. They squealed and dashed after it, having a quite lively and noisy time. Maury wondered what it would be like when Little Al was big enough to play with other kids like that. Then for an awkward moment, he considered whether he would even be around for that. He hoped so and made a little vow to take better care of himself, maybe even to exercise more regularly.

He got back to Fergie's car in plenty of time to slip inside and watch the building's front. If either of the two went back out after getting home from work, he figured he could follow them and see what he could learn about their night life. He'd taken a good look at their photos and listened to Fergie's description of what they were wearing.

The one they called Wacky Jacky, Jacqueline Frineman, was the first to come trudging home after a long day on her feet, waiting tables and probably doing much of the bussing in the sort of tiny diner Fergie had described. Maury had a hunch she wasn't going to go out anywhere that evening. She seemed barely able to make it up the front stairs.

He was pouring himself a cup of coffee from a thermos when Kristina Smeerna finally appeared on the street. Before she went up the stairs, she glanced over at Fergie's car. Maury hadn't expected that, and it was too late to duck beneath the dash. She glared at him then flipped him the bird, giving him the same treatment she'd offered Fergie.

Maury sat in the car, mulling over whether staying on to see if they went anywhere that evening was going to be worthwhile. Barely twenty minutes later, a big guy with closely cropped gray hair and wearing a royal-blue jacket that might just hide a shoulder holster walked deliberately toward Maury.

He came up to the driver's side of the car and signaled for Maury to roll down the window.

As soon as he did, the guy leaned closer, looked him over and said, "What're you up to?"

"Just sitting here. Why?"

"I don't believe you."

"There's no law against sitting in a car, is there?"

"There's a law against stalking."

"Really?" Maury thought he could hear himself swallow.

The guy leaned even closer, until his face was only a couple of inches from Maury's. It wasn't the kind of face Maury would ever want to wake up next to. The man frowned even more intensely. He slowly reached inside the jacket. Maury winced. But instead of a gun, he held out a black leather folder. He flipped it open and let Maury see a gold sheriff's department badge. "I think you'd better scram."

"Yes, sir." Maury thought for a flash of a second of mentioning that he was in the jurisdiction of the city police, but the man's expression, along with the chance a gun was still hidden by that jacket, encouraged him to keep his lips zipped.

Maury started the car, put it in gear, and eased out of the parking space. He was half a dozen blocks away before he took a really good breath. He pulled over and called Al.

"If I give you a sheriff's department badge number, can you find out who it belongs to?"

"Sure. I can call Clayton. Why?"

"I just got the bum's rush from someone with a gold one."

"Uh-oh."

"Is it all quiet out there?"

"It is now if you don't count someone unloading an Uzi in Fergie's direction a short while ago."

"Sounds like our tiny little trespassing issue is escalating."

"Indeed it is."

Chapter Fourteen

Al and Fergie stood in front of the house, talking to Deputy Waylan. The sky was dark except where the red and blue swirls of light from an SUV cruiser swept across trees and the front of the house. A light breeze swept across them, but it felt as dry as the breath of a desert and smelled of dried brown leaves and grass.

"Are you sure it was an Uzi you heard?" Waylan was a slim middle-aged deputy with just the beginning of a little round paunch of a stomach. He was going to have to get his uniform altered pretty soon or pop out of it. As it was, his buttons were stretched to the limit at his waist. He was one of those men who chew gum with an energetic and exaggerated enthusiasm, a little open-mouthed and as if trying to bite the gum in half with each chew. Al had been fixated on the spectacle of such jaw gnashing and had to force himself to look away.

"I know what an Uzi sounds like. I've fired one a few times myself, and this wasn't the first time one was fired at me," Fergie said.

The deputy had pretty much completed his report of the trespassing on the property and Fergie getting shot at and was just crossing the t's and dotting the i's.

"There were four of them, but they took off in two different directions." She was staring at Waylan's hard-working jaw and looked half hypnotized by the rhythmic nonstop motion.

Waylan shook his head. "This is just getting more tangled."

As he spoke, a dark-blue Subaru Ascent pulled up the lane and parked beside the cruiser.

"Now, who the hell could that be?" Waylan said.

The headlights went off, and Sheriff Clayton climbed out from the driver's side.

Waylan's mouth snapped all the way open, and his gum fell out.

The county's sheriff's department was a good-sized outfit, with majors, captains, lieutenants, and, of course, quite a few deputies. Leaving his office was a rare occurrence for the sheriff, which was what made his personal visit to see Al unusual in a memorable way.

Clayton came lumbering toward them.

Waylan snapped his black leather notebook closed. "That should do it."

"You all done here?" Clayton asked Waylan as he came up to them.

"Yes, sir. I was just about to make tracks." He headed toward his lit-up cruiser at a brisk pace.

As the cruiser's flashing lights went off, it backed up the lane heading toward the road, and Clayton turned toward Al and Fergie.

"I take it you got something from the badge number I sent you," Al said.

"I did indeed." He glanced at Fergie. "You made some real progress, but I can't say it's all happy news."

Al waited, so Clayton went on. "The badge belongs to Nelson Jeremiah. You know him."

"I do. He's an ambitious fellow. He hasn't made a try at defenestrating you yet, has he?"

"He's announced that he plans to run against me in the coming election."

"That makes him motivated when it comes to any kind of scandal, doesn't it?" Fergie asked.

"I'd say very. But you haven't found him with his hand in the cookie jar yet, just approximate to those two blasted women stirring up this mess."

"You drove all the way out here just to share that?"

"I didn't want anyone at the office to hear me or anyone at home either."

"Oh." Al glanced toward Fergie.

She was looking down but knew as he did that Clayton had been married for well over forty years. So, if the story had any truth to it, Clayton had been married at the time it happened. Al couldn't imagine Clayton doing what those women claimed. Unfounded though it might be, the accusation alone would be poison.

"Bess doesn't know about this?" Al asked.

"No, and I don't want her to know. I'd like to get this all cleared up before it gets blasted all over the media."

"We understand," Fergie said. "I don't suppose you intend to confront Nelson, do you?"

"Not for now, but I'll surely keep an eye on him. You helped quite a bit on that front. But do keep at this chore. I don't have to tell you how very much I appreciate your help."

That must have been hard to say. Al nodded.

Clayton spun and headed toward his vehicle.

Al watched him walk and shook his head. *Damned if he doesn't even walk like John Wayne.*

When he and Fergie went inside, the lights were on, and Bonnie sat at the table, holding an empty mug. "Well?"

"Clayton thinks we're starting to get somewhere with his problem," Fergie told her.

"Well, good for him. That doesn't really help us with unwelcome visitors square-dancing across the property every night and firing guns too," Bonnie said.

"Into each life some rain must fall. We're lucky Fergie didn't get hit by a stray bullet." Al glanced toward the pot of coffee on the stove and decided he didn't want a cup at going on two in the morning. "We'll all just have to stay alert around here for a spell."

"And I'll do what I can to find out more about the two women," Fergie said, "but they're sure not the friendliest birds I've come across, and now that we know they're friends with a well-placed sheriff's department deputy, I'll have to be even more careful."

"Yeah, but I don't think he can arrest you," Bonnie said, "though he might just shoot you."

"Always something to look forward to," Fergie said. With Al, she headed for their bedroom.

THE SUN WAS JUST BEGINNING to rise as Moog sat fuming in the back of his battleship-gray Lincoln Town Car while Fenster drove. Moog liked to sleep in until ten, eleven, or sometimes noon. That, he felt, was the prerogative of a wheeler-dealer like himself. But he'd been summoned. He sure didn't want to go, but he *had* to go. He usually preferred to be the person in control. Life was an ocean of fish, each little one being eaten by a bigger one, and that one harassed by an even bigger one. So there he was, riding along at nearly seven in the morning to go to a breakfast where he probably wouldn't get to eat.

Fenster parked in the back of the parking lot at McAllister's and stayed in the car while Moog went in alone. The walk across the parking lot felt like a long one, and pushing in the thick oak door edged in wrought-iron scrollwork was no easy task either. He could think of any number of places he'd rather be.

The insides of the Victorian-styled restaurant were dimly lit, which catered to a certain sort of clientele. Moog waved off a server who had emerged from the kitchen to hurry toward him with a white towel over one forearm. Moog knew where to go.

Once past the tables near a bar along the right, he entered a narrow hallway with booths along the left. In the far back booth sat two men.

Moog felt himself shudder slightly. He got to the table, and the man facing him, Semion Kashov, looked up at him.

"Don't bother to sit down. You won't be staying long."

"Okay." That was fine with Moog. He would have rather been anywhere but where he stood.

"I'm surprised you're wearing long pants."

"Why's that?"

"Because you had a little case of the shorts."

"Just a few thou."

"Yet the missing part isn't yours. It's mine. You see, you let a thousand slip here and a thousand there, and it starts to turn into real money. I've adopted sort of an iron-fist-in-an-iron-glove policy about such matters."

"I'll get it. A couple of guys…"

Semion glanced at his watch and looked back up. "Is there a story? Make it quick."

The man across the table hadn't looked up but had continued to cut away at a plate of steak and eggs. Moog knew the man only enough to call him Brick and to stay the hell away from him. His large blockish head was covered with a thick mat of black hair, bushy black eyebrows, and a five- to six-day growth of black beard.

"These two guys were supposed to cough up five grand or at least the vig. But they took a flyer on me. They claimed they were going to pay, and soon, so I sent a couple of my guys to see what they were up to since some loose money might be involved."

"And?"

"There's a property out by the lake where they all ended up. There was some shooting."

"But nobody got hurt?"

"Well, Rueben took a rifle shot to the ass the night before."

Semion suppressed a laugh but nearly choked. Brick's shoulders were bouncing up and down a little, like the way Jay Leno used to laugh.

"What is it all about, this money?"

"I have no idea, but it must be worth defending."

"I'll tell you what. You find out what it is, and I get cut in on it."

"I don't know if…"

"Just to make sure you don't forget or somethin', Brick is gonna go with you."

Brick shrugged, tossed his knife and fork onto his plate, and stood up. His face ended up inches from Moog's, who didn't care at all for the blank stare of those eyes, which may have been a very dark brown but looked as black as obsidian up close. Moreover, they looked lifeless and dispassionate, eyes that had never shown emotions like affection or caring, ever. This was a man who had killed and had done so lightly.

"Okay." Moog's voice had gone up an octave and came out as a half squeak.

He turned and could feel the presence of Brick following him closely. An already not-cheerful day had just taken a dark turn.

Brick rode up in the front seat beside Fenster. As they pulled out of the parking lot, Fenster asked, "What sort of work do you do for Mister Kashov?"

"Mostly knife work, some guns, and… cleanup."

"Cleanup?"

"You know. Body removal and such."

The rest of the ride back to Moog's place was silent.

"WHERE ARE WE GOING?" Budge asked.

"Do you see where the needle is on our gas gauge?" Griff kept his eyes on the two-lane road but nodded quickly toward the dash.

"Yeah. I'm not blind. We're almost empty. That's not what I asked you."

Griff had noticed Budge getting gradually snippier as time went by without a meal or any hope for one.

Woods crowded the road on each side, with occasional breaks for a pasture here and there, where cattle stood in small groups or, in one farmyard, a single white horse stared out across a three-wire fence at where they passed by. A whiff of grass so dry it smelled like straw mingled with the earthy livestock droppings, reminding Griff of a childhood where his ma had made him wear bib overalls and do chores like some hired hand while his father dressed up in the best finery he owned and went out to call square dances and play a fiddle. Acting the part of a city-bred dandy was always a stretch for Griff but worth the effort when he turned some young lady's head.

"There's a woman I know who lives out this way."

"You were always better around women than me."

"It's like a radio, Budge. You just keep twiddling with the dials until you get a good station."

"Does this one have a friend?"

"It's not that kind of deal. We're going to wait until she leaves the house."

"Aw, man."

"It's like that," Griff said, "unless you've got another idea for how to get money quickly, not to mention food."

He knew he had Budge's attention when he mentioned food.

"We'll see how this goes," Budge grumped.

Griff could tell he was thinking about food. To stoke Budge's big furnace of a stomach took plenty of the stuff.

Ahead, he saw the twin ruts of a rough-and-tumble dirt road that turned into a vacant, overgrown pasture. He bumped and bounced along until he was way back from the road and out of sight.

"Now what?" Budge asked.

"We take a short hike and then wait. It's almost eleven, and she'll be heading out for noon bingo at her church."

"Oh, man. She's a churchgoer too."

"Mostly just for the bingo, I think."

"Still."

"Focus on food, big guy, and how much we need it and want it."

Griff tucked the truck back between a couple of trees and behind a chest-high wall of prickly pear cactus.

"We gonna need anything from the truck?" Budge asked.

"Just ourselves."

They climbed out of the truck, Griff in his corduroy slacks, which were far too tattered for him to be seen in public wearing them. But they'd be okay for the job at hand.

Budge bent to look at his reflection in the window of the truck. He took out a comb missing only a few teeth and combed his mullet into place—all business in the front and the-hell-with-you in the back, a Southern boy's charm.

Griff tried not to think of the sights and smells he recalled from working in the area. He had once worked on a pig farm, hired out as a hand on loan by his father, who needed the money. Slave labor wasn't something mentioned in their house. Everyone had to pitch in or get out, which was exactly what Griff did when he graduated high school at seventeen. He hadn't turned into anything like a whopping success, but he was his own man, and no one could take that away from him.

That time slogging around in a giant pigsty of a farm had put him off the notion of ever doing hard work for money again. Horse poop, he could stand and almost enjoy. Cow poop, he could endure. But pig poop? *Oink!* He had never felt anywhere close to good about it—would have been quite put off hogs altogether if it hadn't been for ham and Swiss on rye with a really dark spicy mustard. *Dammit, I'm thinking about food again.*

Budge trailed close behind him as Griff followed a deer path to the property's barbed-wire fence. He climbed over and led the way to a thick green cluster of mountain cedar that hadn't yet started showing the effects of drought. They crowded into a flattened area in the middle, where deer had hunkered down and made it a smooth bed of dried reddish-orange cedar leaves.

Griff moved a cedar limb and peeked around it.

"That's one tiny little cabin." Budge nearly pressed against Griff as he took a look too.

"Now we wait." Griff glanced at his watch. *Damn.* It was one good-looking watch even if it was a knockoff. "She'll be heading for bingo any time now."

As if on cue, a tiny woman with a white Q-tip hairdo emerged from the front door, locked it, and headed for the worn little black 2003 Kia Rio sedan covered in a light layer of dust and occasional small dents. She headed off down her dirt lane, her ears probably already hearing the call of B-15 or G-56.

As soon as the car was out of sight, Griff pushed out from the thick green limbs and started for the cabin.

"I don't like this," Budge said. "It's a little old lady with probably little money."

"We'll pay her back when we have the gold."

"We'd better."

When he got to the front door, Griff slowed and looked around. There it was. A little plastic almost realistic rock among the stones surrounding a bed of white vinca blooms, around which the ground was wet, testifying to the woman's efforts to help them survive in the existing arid conditions.

Griff lifted the fake rock and took out a key. "I knew one guy who would put his key-holding phony-baloney stone right on the porch because he was afraid he couldn't find it if he mixed it in with others in a rock garden."

He unlocked the front door, and they both slipped inside as quickly as they could. A *grrr* sounded from a corner of a small couch, and a light-brown ball of fur shot toward them, the Chihuahua barking away as it crossed the room in a dead run, its teeth snapping as it barked.

As soon as it got toward them it went for the biggest of them, Budge, and latched onto the pants cuff of his jeans and wouldn't let go. It shook its head and growled, "Rrr, rrr, rrr."

Griff saw the dog's name spelled out on his collar: "Chico."

He reached for the dog, but it swiveled away, keeping an eye on him while not letting go of the pant leg.

"Turn this way, so I can kick him off you," Griff said.

Budge's voice lowered an octave in stern warning as he said, "I want to make one thing perfectly clear to you, Griff. Anything you do to this little dog, I'm going to do to you. Are we clear on that?"

"What?"

"Are we clear?" Budge shouted.

Griff looked up from the dog to Budge's eyes. He'd forgotten for just a silly, stupid moment how Budge felt about dogs.

"We're clear," he said in a small voice. He looked away. "Now, help me look around."

Budge headed for the small kitchen, gently dragging the tiny dog along, its tail wagging vigorously as it growled and tugged at the denim.

The living room was sparsely furnished. It looked like the couch folded out into a bed each night. The damned little dog probably slept on it with her.

A small television and a few weathered copies of *Reader's Digest* on a side table were all he could see in that room. So he went to the kitchen, where Budge had half a slice of bologna hanging from his mouth and was holding out another bit of it to the dog. Chico let go of the pant leg long enough to grab the offered treat and bolt it down then went right back to his death grip on Budge's jeans. Budge didn't try to stop it, and Griff sure didn't after that brief caution from Budge.

Griff's eyes swept the room. A kettle was resting on the stove, and a cheap brown ceramic teapot sat on the table beside an almost matching teacup. Another slightly cracked green teapot sat on top of the fridge. That would be the place.

Budge took just enough from the fridge to make a couple of sandwiches. The little old lady was probably one of those who carefully made purchases at the grocery and paid in counted change.

Griff reached for the green teapot, lifted off the lid, and brought out a roll of mostly small bills: twenties, tens, and even quite a few ones—a poor person's stash. When he counted out the wad, it came to two hundred and eleven dollars. Griff started to put it all in his pocket.

"Leave her some," Budge said.

"Don't forget how desperate we are to get some money... or food."

"It's all she has."

Griff looked at him. Those eyes were glittering again, the eyebrows bunched in a frown.

He put some of it back in the teapot, mostly the ones.

Budge gently dragged Chico along toward the front door. "You go out first, and I'll let the little guy loose and make a dash myself," Budge said. He reached down for the little dog and pulled it free from his leg, not even wincing when it sank its teeth between the first finger and thumb.

While Budge was otherwise occupied, Griff quickly took the rest of the cash back out of the teapot, slipped it into his pocket, and hurried over to the front door.

He went out first, and Budge was right behind him, closing the door on the snarling, barking Chico.

Griff glanced at the small line of bleeding holes on Budge's hand.

Budge took out a handkerchief and wrapped it around the wounded area. "He was just doing his job, the cute little fellow. I sure hope the tiny old gal forgives him for letting the place get robbed a bit."

Chapter Fifteen

As Fergie drove out the lane, she had to pull over to the right halfway down to let two vehicles pass. Both Dirty Fingernails Huff and Meat Jenkins waved at her as they went by. Jenkins drove a sparkling-clean black Jeep and was the IT expert for the sheriff's department, but he'd helped Al in the past with one or two little techie issues, for which he was usually paid in something sweet that probably went dead against whatever diet he was on at the moment to counter his growing bulk. That must have been why Fergie had been asked to pick up a turtle cheesecake on her way home. Huff's vehicle was a creaking gray Ford Ranger with a homemade wooden shed resting on its bed. Fergie thought she saw the glittering eyes of a critter of some sort peeking out a window of the shed, which could've been a ferret, raccoon, or any of a number of other wildlife that followed him around. In addition to being at one with nature, he was an expert on electronics and gadgetry, much like Meat Jenkins. Al hadn't shared with her that they were coming or what he would ask of them. Perhaps it would be better if she didn't know.

She felt glad to know extra folks would be on the property while she was away. They were all getting a little worn down by having to be constantly on their guard against whatever the hell was going on. That was the worst, having no clue about why they'd suddenly been selected for this jackpot of invasive behavior.

Maybe she could make some headway on Clayton's problem so that she could at least stay home and keep a watch over the place. How peaceful and quiet their home had seemed just a week before. Since then, they had all been on edge, except Little Al, who was too young to have any idea they were threatened. Even Tanner was being extra watchful, going to the doors and sniffing as though to detect danger. Al and she had tried and tried to get Bonnie to bundle up Little Al and go somewhere with him and be safe until Bonnie was almost in tears, as if they were asking her to be something she was not. In the end, they'd had to respect the person she was, who would have felt diminished if she couldn't stay and do her part in the home defense. Perhaps that was just as well, since she was the best shot of them, but Fergie and Al would feel terrible if anything happened to Little Al.

Her stomach was a knot of tension as Fergie drove into town to do the poking she had set up with several phone calls. To keep her mind open, clear, and objective, she focused on the scenery she passed. Where hillsides had once been green with tall grass and late wildflowers, yellow and brown waves swayed in the breeze. Even the trees were showing stress, and vines had become dark-brown strings of lights on the cedars.

Traffic had become its usual tangled knot, reminding Fergie of earlier days when she could drive about effortlessly through the town. But thinking about those times only pounded in the nail that she was in her sixties and retired. The world was changing all around her. She could dig in her heels and try to make it slow down, but that was as useless as trying to saddle a pig.

She let her GPS do the work of finding the house she sought, nearly a bungalow of a cottage in South Austin, an area that natives called Bubba Land. The people there were in general more laid back, some still living the hippie-dippie days with incense, candles, and even a few lava lamps, not to mention the odd hookah lying about.

The houses had gotten smaller, the yards more cluttered, and the narrow streets lined with parked cars from who-knew-how-many people living together in the crowded houses. She had to park a block and a half away and walk back to the tiny home. Small flagstones formed a path from the sidewalk to the front door, and it was lined by plants that had been blooming once but had begun to wither, with only a few marigolds that needed deadheading remaining. The small bits of yellowish lawn didn't need mowing and would probably sound like Rice Krispies if walked upon.

The house's exterior was made of the sort of siding shingles Fergie thought used to be made of asbestos, and they'd been painted a darkish hunter green. The front door, covered with chipped red paint, had a small square of stained glass at eye level. The doorbell hung loose by one wire at one side of the door, so Fergie knocked.

The woman who swung the door open had white bed hair that looked like Einstein had just put his finger in a socket. A nonfilter cigarette hung from her lower lip in a face as wrinkled as a topographical map. She wore a blue flannel robe over frumpy pink pajamas frayed at the collar and ankle hems. One of the ears had fallen off her fluffy pink bunny slippers.

"C'mon in. I'm not really dressed to receive, but what the hell."

She closed her lips on the cigarette, and the end flared red. Two forced flumes of smoke shot downward from her nostrils.

"Elizabeth McHiggins?" Fergie asked as she stepped inside.

"None other, though friends call me Lizzie. You know, like the ax lady."

"Really?"

The living room had all the blinds and curtains pulled shut, and with the cigarette smoke, current and previous, the room felt stuffy. An overstuffed recliner covered with an orange-and-brown cloth sat facing a television resting on an entertainment table in one corner of the room. Lizzie sat down on one end of a darker-brown couch and waved a hand toward the other end.

Fergie brushed a few cat hairs away and sat down.

An ashtray filled to overflowing sat on the end table beside Lizzie, next to a plain white coffee mug and a bottle of cheap gin.

From her digging, Fergie knew she and Lizzie were about the same age, but Lizzie looked twenty or thirty years older.

Lizzie poured some of the gin into the coffee mug and glanced toward Fergie. "Do you want any coffee?"

Fergie didn't see a coffee pot or thermos nearby. "No. I had plenty with breakfast," she said, realizing that Lizzie had probably not had a breakfast but had started her day pretty much as it was going at the moment, with liquor and cigarettes.

"Ms. McHiggins—"

"Lizzie."

"Okay, Lizzie, you are the person who ran a camp where Girl Scouts once went to for a summer camp, aren't you?"

"Well, all kinds attended that place: church groups, Boy Scouts, band camps, recovering lushes, and yeah, Girl Scouts."

"I want to ask you about something that may have happened thirty years ago."

"Oh, lordy. I can barely recall what happened yesterday. The years have beaten up on me considerable. But take your shot."

"Would you have been aware of it if any people staying at the camp ever fooled around?"

That made Lizzie start laughing so hard that she shifted into a coughing fit and had to put out her cigarette and reach for a tissue.

Fergie didn't know whether she should go over and pat her on the back or just leave her alone to get over the bout.

After a good five minutes, Lizzie blew her nose, took a deep drink from her mug, and reached for the pack of Camels next to the ashtray. "Oh, land. You got me reliving some scraps of the past with that."

"So there was some fooling around?"

"Ha. I'll say." Lizzie squinted at Fergie through a cloud of smoke in front of her face, one eye nearly closed. "Mind you, ninety-nine percent of those coming to the camp were disinterested in that or had a rigid working moral compass. For just a few of the others, it could be like Gomorrah and that other place."

"Really?" Fergie recalled a conversation she'd had with Al where they had both reluctantly admitted they had graduated from high school as seventeen-year-old virgins.

"Well, you take a bunch of young bodies that are beginning to change and have fresh, new, hard-to-understand urges and mix them into the temptation of being away from home and around each other, you're gonna get one or two experimenters."

"Even the Girl Scouts?"

"You hear of that book *Lolita*?"

"Yeah."

"Well, like that."

"Hmm."

"And I'll tell you what, some of them church groups sure had one or two rotten apples in the barrel. You suppress emotions too long, and it's just like dynamite. It'll blow up."

"Did you ever catch any of them at anything or see or hear anything?"

"Oh, I heard all kinds o' stuff. But I was more than halfway encouraged to look the other way, let people be as long as no one was gettin' hurt."

"Do you know how I might go about finding out who was visiting the camp, say, on July seventh thirty years ago?"

That nearly sent Lizzie off into another fit of coughing. She sure could laugh heartily. "I can barely remember last week. As for any records, I think they burned all of that when they closed the camp down half a dozen years ago. No one wanted anyone mucking around with what was done and done in the past, I guess."

Fergie realized she was at a dead end. Lizzie would be an unreliable witness and, for the life of her, couldn't remember anything anyway. Fergie glanced at the gin bottle and had an idea about that.

"I guess that's it," Fergie said. "I appreciate your time and what you could share."

Lizzie shook her head. "Was nice havin' you drop by. I don't get much company. But now, I'm sussing up to take a morning power nap if that's okay with you."

"Fine, just fine with me," Fergie said, heading for the door, eager to catch a breath of fresh air.

She had no one else to go to and no one to see, and she would have been hard pressed to say she'd been any kind of successful. Fergie didn't turn on the radio or even hum to herself on the way home although she had an earworm or two playing background music in her head. She watched rows and rows of new houses going up in land that had once been all green, and she added up all she had learned so far. As Bonnie might have put it, she had diddly damn squat.

MEAT JENKINS HAD JUST shown Al and Maury how to make sense of the images they were going to see on their television screen and was turning to take Maury outside to field test running a drone when Huff opened the front door with a ferret on his shoulder.

"Hey, Al, I found a coon on your land while I was poking around the way you asked, and it said it wouldn't mind coming home with me for a spell." Huff had somehow gotten a smear of what Al hoped was mud across one cheek and his forehead. He certainly wasn't willing to do anything like a scratch-and-sniff test to find out exactly what it was.

"Is it tame?"

"Mostly. I had to convince it a bit to get it in a crate, but it's ready to roll if you say okay."

"Sure. Okay. There's a porcupine and a couple of skunks that come square-dancing through every now and again. You're welcome to them too if you like."

"I'm not ready to wrassle the likes of them today or have a go at a bobcat either. That coon pitched me enough attitude for one day while I was rounding it up."

"I'm glad you got the best of it."

"It was nip and tuck there for a spell, but you know me. I can be convincing when it comes to critters."

"I have never had the slightest reason to disbelieve that, Huff."

"You need any help with that rascal?" Bonnie called up from downstairs, where she was watching Little Al.

"Naw. I'll be fine. I've got the best of bigger fellers than this and tamed 'em in pretty short order." He was always wary of mentioning raccoons around Bonnie, knowing that her pappy used to hunt them and not so he could make them into pets but to put them on the table, cooked along with some corn pone.

Huff wore faded bib overalls that looked like he'd slept in them—probably had. Something was squirming in one of the pockets, but Al decided not to ask and possibly have whatever it was running loose in the house.

"Thanks for everything." Al gave a short wave.

Huff nodded and closed the door behind himself as he faded out the doorway. Al noticed Tanner hadn't even risen to go have a sniff at Huff, had probably gotten enough from across the room.

Al shook his head and went back to checking out the TV screen, making sure he remembered everything Meat Jenkins had shared with them.

AS FERGIE TURNED INTO the lane to their home, Meat Jenkins's jeep was coming toward her. She eased her car over and slowed to a stop.

He pulled up, window to window. Meat was grinning like he'd been up to all kinds of mischief.

She reached over, got a turtle cheesecake in a box out of a bag, and handed it over to him.

He took it lovingly into his vehicle, as carefully as a quarterback with a football. "Thanks ever so much. You saved my life."

Probably giving you diabetes, she thought, but she smiled and waved as he pulled away.

Next, Huff's old Ranger puttered and popped past her, him grinning as well. That time, there was definitely a possum sitting on his left shoulder, trying to reach to the wheel to help steer. It grinned at her as well.

If I had to describe my life to anyone, she thought, *I doubt they'd believe a word I said.*

Once inside the house, Fergie looked around at what on any other day would be a cozy family time. Bonnie was cleaning and polishing the stove while Maury held Little Al on the couch. Tanner was curled up at Al's feet, where he sat at the dining table with a mug within reach. Al held a brush and was stroking it along Tanner's sides and back. The dog's head was raised, and his eyes rolled back in what passed for dog ecstasy.

"You learn anything?" Al asked.

Fergie shook her head and went to pour herself a cup of coffee into a white mug with black letters that said, There's a Chance This Is Tequila. She took a sip. "All I got were bits and pieces, but nothing that fixes the problem. What were Huff and Meat Jenkins up to? Same sort of thing as last time we had knuckleheads invading the property?"

"No. Huff said no more holes and tripwires this time," Al said. "They both came up with something different and new this time. Huff says he doesn't want to harm a single critter. He had to rescue a few members of our wildlife the last time."

"All you have to do to get a raccoon out of a deep hole is let down a rope ladder, and it'll coon out on its own." Bonnie grinned at the image she'd presented.

"How about skunks?" Fergie asked.

"Yeah, there's that," Bonnie said. "Huff didn't want any excited does running into one of the holes and breaking a leg either. We were lucky last time."

"Well, I for one am glad I missed their visit while I was away," Fergie said. "I don't believe that Huff even bathes."

"I know he doesn't," Al said. "He claims it helps his critters know him."

Bonnie chuckled. "Hell, critters in the next county can tell where he is."

"For that matter, it's always a good idea to sit upwind from Meat Jenkins most of the time." Fergie took a sip of her coffee. After years of police department coffee that could remove shellac, she had to admit that Bonnie could whip up about the best coffee to be had.

It sure felt good to be back around them all, but she had no idea how long the peace and calm would last.

Chapter Sixteen

Fenster flinched as the others clambered into Moog's battleship-gray Lincoln Town Car that he kept detailed spic-and-span and halfway thought of as his own after chauffeuring Moog around in it for going on three years. Ike and Rueben got into the back, the latter more slowly since he had to sit on an inflatable doughnut of a cushion. Brick slid into the front passenger seat. Fenster sighed and got into the driver's seat and started the car. He hadn't been keen to have Brick know where Moog's house was, in the Tarrytown area of mid-Austin among the homes of professors, but chances were Semion Kashov knew every little detail about Moog's life.

Rush hour was going on in Austin, which wasn't much different than a herd of metal cattle pouring through the streets one way and another. Fenster's days as a getaway driver had prepared him for taking off like a bolt of blue, but he'd had to slowly learn the Novocain-like calm of taxi drivers who rarely seemed to let nearby antics fluster them.

When he got the car up to Thirty-Eighth Street, he slid in between a UPS truck and a slow-moving Volvo. "Where to?"

"Head to southeast Austin," Rueben said. "I know a wrecking yard there that's a bit loosey-goosey about taking the plates off incoming vehicles."

Fenster drove through some neighborhoods that made him check to ensure the doors were all locked. Ramshackle little homes sat next to single-wide trailers up on cement blocks. Some doors stood open, and the occasional resident sat in the doorway, looking out at the world passing by. Tiny bodegas sat on the corners of several blocks, places where locals could easily walk to pick up a few essentials like pinto beans, corn husks, or Jarritos sodas. The sound of airplanes roaring louder overhead meant they were getting closer to the Austin-Bergstrom International Airport. Accompanying that, from his cracked window top, he could hear the strains of an overloud mariachi band's music playing. Ike and Rueben gave him directions as he drove. They passed a Latino nightclub where, Fenster had heard in the news, a knifing had happened only a few days before. The sky was getting gradually darker, and he wondered what a night spot looked like when it was really hopping, with cars and trucks parked until they filled the parking lot, people coming and going, some leaning against vehicles and smoking or drinking.

"One more left just ahead," Rueben said.

A high chain-link fence ran the length of the long property, with huge flaps of sheet metal painted green covering some stretches. Every once in a while, a sign said Eddie Paul's Wrecks.

"Stop here," Ike said when they were midway along the side. He took a small wrench out of a long side pocket in his jeans, got out of the car, looked around, and slipped across the street.

"Do these guys always carry car-boosting gear on them?" Brick asked.

"As far as I know, yes," Fenster said.

Rueben nodded. "You never know when opportunity is gonna knock."

Fenster watched Ike pry a flap of the green metal out and slip inside under it. "I guess you can't just use the front door."

"Not and help yourself to free stuff," Rueben said.

While they sat and waited, a boy on a bicycle rolled up next to the car. He had his black hoodie pulled up over his head with the strings tied tight. He turned his head to give the car a threatening glare, but whatever he saw in the front passenger seat made him rock his head back and pedal away as fast as he could go.

Barely ten minutes later, Ike popped back out of the flap he'd used, looked around, and came scurrying back, carrying a pair of license plates in one hand. He got into the back seat. "Hit it, wheelman," he said, having learned a bit of Fenster's past.

As the beginning of evening was setting in, rush hour was doing its damnedest, and the residential streets they drove through in South Austin were still quiet. Ike and Rueben were eager to demonstrate the car-boosting skills that had gotten them kicked out of high school and sent to juvie. They had Fenster drive around through some of the calmest and drowsiest neighborhoods until they spotted a white 2006 Ford 150 with an extended cab, one of the most stolen vehicles in all of Texas and one in which they could all be comfortable. Ike looked at the surrounding houses, all with blinds and shades down against the heat, and climbed out of the car to scamper to the target truck from half a block away. He took a slim jim from the same side pocket in his jeans where he'd carried the wrench and was inside in seconds. He was soon behind them in order to follow. Fenster drove Moog's car back where it belonged so that they could all switch to the truck and be on their mission.

"Didn't even have to hotwire it," Ike said, when he handed a key over to Fenster. "Damn fool kept a spare key behind the visor. It's usually that or the glove box."

They climbed into the stolen truck, Brick in the front seat beside Fenster, the other two in the back seat.

Fenster was uncomfortable driving a stolen vehicle even if Ike had switched the plates and the ride shouldn't draw any heat. In all his years of driving getaway vehicles, he'd never felt good about grand theft auto being added to an abetting charge. On the other hand, he certainly didn't want the current lot of passengers to be riding any longer than they had to in Moog's battleship-gray Lincoln Town Car.

"How far out of town is this property?" Brick asked. He still sat in the front passenger seat, with Ike and Rueben in the back. He hadn't spoken much, but when he did, his voice rumbled like a storm about to happen, and a threat lay behind every word.

"Not all that far. We're nearly there."

Fenster didn't mind goons like Ike and Rueben, petty lifelong criminals willing do anything but go back to some jail or other. But Brick was a shark in shallow water. Just a glance his way made Fenster's insides twitchy. He knew he'd made so many kills that he'd probably lost count. His dark-brown eyes had the blank, emotionless stare of a psychotic predator. Fenster hadn't been able to maintain eye contact for more than a few seconds at any time.

As they got close to the property, Fenster said, "These other guys don't think we know where they park, but I have a pretty good hunch, judging from the direction they ran when someone started shooting."

"There's gonna be a little gunplay?" Something like the beginning of a smile flickered across Brick's face.

"Might be. If so, it's you guys doing it, not me," Fenster said.

They went past a couple of properties with homes facing the lake until they came to a more run-down lot. If it had a For Sale sign, someone had knocked it down, but it didn't look occupied.

Fenster turned into the lane, pleased to see tire tracks on the twin dirt ruts.

Coming around a thick copse of trees and brush, the truck's headlights swept over a red truck parked ahead of them.

"If they're in there, you can put the grab on them. But if they've already gone onto the property, you'll have to follow them to make any kind of snatch."

Ike and Brick softly and quietly eased up to the truck, looked in, and shook their heads. Rueben was still slowly making his way out of the back seat. He waved back to Fenster as he, Ike, and Brick moved forward and out of sight into the dark.

Fenster turned off the truck's lights, rolled down his window, and turned off the engine. He sat listening to the sounds of the night around him. Wind rustled the high tops of the trees. Some kind of bird was making a fuss not too far away. And the truck's engine made an occasional pop or ping as it cooled.

GRIFF AND BUDGE MOVED as quietly as they could, Griff at least. Budge, try as he might, made cracks, crackles, and pops with every step. Dark as it had gotten under the umbrella of treetops, they stayed close together. Budge carried the metal detector.

Brushing up against an agarita bush, Griff felt its stiff, sharp holly-like leaves grab at his new pants. "Oh crap. I should have worn the tattered pair."

With the newfound money, they had shopped, Budge getting a loaf of bread, thick-sliced bologna, and a small bottle of ketchup at an HEB grocery, where the prices were better than in convenience stores. Once they bought some gas, Griff went to three thrift shops before he could find anything close to replacing the clone version of Todd Snyder corduroy slacks he felt he had to have to look properly dapper.

Two steps more, and a mesquite branch grabbed at Griff's slacks. "Aw, man. I'm gonna ruin these. I just paid seven dollars for them." That was more than he had paid for their groceries since he said they needed to go light. "Let's go back to the truck for just a sec, and let me switch out pants. The other ones are already buggered up."

"We haven't swept this corner of the place," Budge said. "Why don't you go while I get a start on looking for that gold?"

For a second, Griff wondered if Budge wanted all the gold for himself, but that was his own greed talking. What could Budge do if he did locate the treasure? They would have to work together to get it out.

"Okay. I'll be right back as soon as I can."

BUDGE WAITED AND LISTENED. As soon as he could no longer hear Griff's careful steps, he reached into his shirt pocket and took out a sandwich bag that held three slices of extra-thick bologna on white bread with lots of ketchup. They had gotten the cheapest dollar-a-loaf bread they could find, but that mattered little to him. All he knew was that he was as hungry as he'd ever been.

AL'S EYES SNAPPED OPEN at the sound of a low *ding, ding, ding,* which was the alarm his two techie friends, Dirty Fingernails Huff and Meat Jenkins, had set up. They hadn't wanted anything too loud and strident, just enough to wake Al, who could sleep like a fireman on duty when he was on edge, as he had been for a while. Tanner stood up and stretched, tail wagging in eagerness as Al and Fergie climbed into their clothes.

They got their pistols and rushed out to the living room, where Maury had already turned on the television. Only two boxes on the screen showed activity. If a trespasser had come from any of eight directions, a motion-detecting infrared camera would have activated, capturing their movement. At the moment, they could see two men entering the property, one carrying a metal detector.

"Them's the ones," Bonnie said, coming up to join them in front of the television. She wore a fuzzy pink bathrobe on which one pocket hung low, probably with her Chiefs Special tucked inside.

"Is one of them the one you shot in the butt?" Fergie asked.

"Nope. Them were two other fellas."

"We sure have them coming out of the woodwork." Fergie shook her head.

"You'd better fire up one of the drones, Maury."

Maury's eyes lit up as he said it. Maury was a fiend for new toys.

"Be careful with that," Al said. "One with a camera like that's got to be worth at least four hundred."

"Oh goodie," Maury mumbled, grabbing one and its control while heading for the front door.

In a moment, a box on the screen lit up and moved briskly as the drone took off at Maury's bidding. Al had to admit that Maury was pretty handy with it, having practiced in the afternoon. The drone wove through trees, and its camera soon picked up a man standing alone with the metal detector. They'd seen the other one head off by himself, going off the property.

Al was about to go to the door and yell for Maury to follow the other one. But Maury had already figured that out, and the drone swept away, lighting up a path. As it swept past the big guy, he spun and took off running in the same direction.

As the drone grew closer, they could make out a couple of vehicles ahead, a red and a white truck, and men beside them. The smaller of the two trespassers was held tightly by two of the men, and they were frog-marching him toward the white truck.

The drone swooped down for a closer look, catching fear and panic on the face of the one being shoved into the back of the truck.

A swarthy dark fellow spun, glared at the drone, and in one motion drew something from inside his jacket and threw it at the drone, which shattered, and the picture was gone in a flash.

"That's some knife throwing, to hit a moving drone in the air," Fergie said.

"I have a feeling these aren't very nice people we're dealing with," Al said.

As he spoke, the big guy with the detector ran out of sight on their television, and that motion detector shut down, and the screen went dark

BUDGE FELT VERY ALONE as he flat out ran as fast as he could, knowing he was making a lot of noise. But there was little he could do about that. Stickers and burrs grabbed at his jeans as he ran, but he ignored them.

He burst into the open near their truck in time to see a white truck pulling away.

"Griff?" he yelled. "Griff!"

Nothing.

"Someone's snatched him." He knew he had little time, and he saw no sense in looking around. Griff had the keys and all their money, but the truck did have gas. He went to the flap over the gas cap and flipped it open, reached up inside, grabbed the black metal box there, and yanked it out. He slid one side open and let the key fall into his hand.

As quickly as he could, he unlocked the truck, slid the metal detector inside, and got into the driver's seat. He took off in a spinning spray of dirt and dried yellow grass, headed out onto the road, and guessing left would be better than right, just took off as fast as he could go before settling into a regular fifty on the forty-five-mile-per-hour road so as not to attract attention. With his window down, he could hear sirens approaching in the distance. At least they seemed to be coming from the other direction.

As Budge drove, he took a quick inventory. He had the metal detector and their two travel bags, along with Griff's garment bag. The rest of the groceries were still in their bag. He had one of the two burner phones they had purchased when they got the detector, so maybe Griff could call him if he was okay. Budge sure hoped Griff was unharmed. Moog was probably behind the snatch. He'd have to wait and see.

When they were constantly together, he'd never thought how much he and Griff depended on each other. As he made a turn into a Walmart parking lot, he was thinking about Griff constantly, hoping he wasn't being hurt, hoping they would be back together again soon. He always heard that Walmart stores let people stay in their lots overnight, especially travelers who might make purchases inside. Budge wasn't one of those. Griff had all the money, and for all he knew, that would be gone by now too.

He parked close enough under a mercury vapor light that splashed a bluish white onto the asphalt so that he could at least read. Before he got out his book, he took the grocery bag and made sandwich after sandwich until all the bologna was gone. He knew he ought to save some, but it wouldn't keep well anyway, and he had a hollow hole where his stomach used to be. So he ate it all. He supposed he could always make ketchup sandwiches the next day since he had half the bread and ketchup left.

Then he got out his book and tried to read but found he couldn't concentrate or see the film of what was happening on the pages in his head. He could only fret about Griff, wondering if he was alive. Finally, he closed the book, left it on his lap, and leaned back in his seat. He blinked and looked out across the largely deserted lot. A single tear started down one cheek. He angrily brushed it away, but another soon followed.

Chapter Seventeen

A couple of deputies were still taking a quick look around Al's property when Victor Kahlon pulled up the drive in an unmarked black SUV. He parked beside one of the cruisers and headed for the house, where Al stood talking to one deputy. He had been promoted to detective after Al left the department, and they'd worked together a number of times since, the only difference being Victor drew a salary. But he wasn't usually out and about at night unless his talents were needed.

When the deputy saw Kahlon, he nodded to Al. "I've got enough for now. You can give anything else to Victor."

"I understand you got some footage of the people tiptoeing about on your property this time," he said as he shook hands with Al.

Al reached into his shirt pocket and took out a flash drive. He handed it over to Kahlon.

"I stopped and took a look at your defense system. Those look a lot like the ones we have in the department."

"They're on loan. Clayton gave the okay."

"I heard you lost a drone as well. One of ours?"

"You're welcome to the pieces. You have a copy of the drone's film too. Helluva thing to hit a drone midair with a throwing knife. I'd give you that, too, if I had it. Whoever threw it apparently went back to be sure and take it with him."

"I imagine I'll be entertained by the films. Do you have any idea of who these people are who keep coming back at you?"

"That's what I'm hoping you can find out with the films. I didn't recognize any of them."

"I'll get on it." Kahlon started to turn to go back to his vehicle but stopped. He looked back. "You have no idea what seems to be bringing this sort of jasper to your place like moths to a flame?"

"Not a clue," Al said. "Maybe when we know who they are."

"I have a gut hunch not even that may help."

"I was a demon with gut hunches back in my day when I was doing the job that you do. Can't say they always panned out. Let's hope we can parse all this out before someone gets hurt."

DRIVING INTO TOWN THE next morning, as soon as the rush-hour craziness had a chance to pass, Fergie doubted her chances but had decided to try and have a chat with the one they called Wacky Jacky.

She parked half a block away from the diner, sauntered down the sidewalk, and went in as though she was a regular customer. Most of the booths were full, and only three seats were left at the counter.

Jacqueline Frineman, Jacky, was pouring coffee from a pot into a counter customer's mug when she saw Fergie. She fumbled with the pot and nearly dropped it. Turning carefully, she put the pot back where it belonged. When she turned back to Fergie, her eyes were narrowed, and one side of her lip was up in a snarl. She practically marched over to Fergie.

"What do you want?"

"This is a diner. Can I get something to eat?" She glanced toward the balding man behind the grill. He was watching them.

"What then?"

"How about oatmeal?"

"That's all?"

"I'd be glad to hear what really happened on June seventh thirty years ago."

Jacky's shoulders tightened, and her eyes opened wide.

"I'd also be glad to know what interest Nelson Jeremiah has in the two of you."

Jacky spun without speaking. She filled a bowl and turned back around. When the guy doing the grilling turned away for a moment, she bent forward and spat into the bowl, making sure Fergie saw her.

She brought the bowl over and slid it in front of Fergie with a smile as genuine as a crocodile's.

"How much?" Fergie had to face it—the trip had been a waste.

Jacky wrote out a bill on a pad from her apron. She slapped it onto the counter. The amount was three dollars and fifty cents.

Fergie put the exact amount onto the bill, and at the bottom, she wrote, "No tip."

She got up and walked back out of the diner. She'd made a long trip to town that had come to nothing. But she had gotten to see Jacky turn a few different colors.

As she walked back to her car, she mentally kicked herself a little. She didn't know if she'd actually expected that Jacky would fess up that the whole thing was a sham. Fergie couldn't trip her up on anything either. The past is hazy at best and more so when some people manipulate it.

She shook her head. "Well, I gave it a shot."

CLAYTON CALLED AL SHORTLY before noon. "Any luck with my little wrinkle?"

"Nope. The two women are tough nuts. I don't think we'll get anywhere with either of them. Have you had a sit-down chat with Nelson Jeremiah yet?"

"Not yet, but he was half a step away from giving me the stink eye today before he thought better of it."

"Have you identified anyone in the films?"

"A couple of them are lowlife types who do some leg work for Moog Palance, a local small-time loan shark. The other two who came in first seem a blank to us, with no sheet or priors that we know of. But let me tell you about the swarthy one."

"Who took out the drone?"

"That's the one. We think he's probably some kind of Russian mafia and is one of only a few people to have a price on his head. A reward for information on him leading to his arrest was offered by the governor of New Mexico. Apparently, a whole family was brutally murdered after the husband's drug connections were exposed. Law enforcement and local governments don't normally do rewards for information, but the wife's father was big in oil and put up the money. The case had been just missing persons until some backcountry prospector came across a burial pit out in the nowhere. When excavated, they found the remains of the father, the wife, two children, and the family dog, a collie. They'd been covered in quicklime, but enough was still there for the identifications. The husband, having been caught in a fentanyl mess himself, was about to give up others. The DEA, thinking they were about to make a major bust, was upset and eager too, but in this case, they weren't the ones putting up a reward."

"So this guy is dangerous?"

"Very."

GRIFF SAT IN THE BACK of the car between two guys, Ike and Rueben. He felt chilled to his bones that they didn't care if he knew their names, nor had they blindfolded him. The driver, Fenster, was going where the swarthy one, Brick, told him to go.

"Empty his pockets, and hand everything up here," Brick said.

They took his switchblade he'd had no chance to use, his burner phone, and the wad of bills he had left.

"Do we all get a share of the cash?" Ike asked as he put everything in Brick's hand.

"Doesn't look that way, does it?" Brick said. "This is no damn democracy."

All of that convinced Griff he was taking his last ride ever. He reviewed the few high points of his life, as well as the lows, of which the current situation was at the top of the list.

The car pulled up outside a chain-link gate at a warehouse. The one called Brick got out and looked around. He unlocked the padlock and waved for them to go through. As soon as Fenster stopped, they hurried out of the truck. The back seat two walked Griff to the door Brick held open, one of them limping profoundly. The interior was dark until one of them flipped a switch and rows of fluorescent lights hanging from the ceiling lit up the insides.

Stacks of boxes crowded the floor of the warehouse, so they had to pass through a narrow maze of the different-sized boxes on pallets. One summer, Griff had worked at a trucking company loading and unloading trucks. What he saw around him was a trip down memory lane, although he doubted he was in a shipping depot, more likely a place where someone stored hijacked loads of goods from semis, given the character of the men holding him and guiding him along. Being allowed to see such a considerable stash of loot troubled him even more deeply since it also underscored that he had slim chances of living through the current mess.

Huge fans high on the walls at either end of the building whirred away, making a steady white noise and stirring the smells of cardboard, dust, and wood.

His mind was racing. Always one to weigh his chances and look for opportunities, he looked around the building and into the eyes of those who held him, losing a little hope when he saw the glitter in Brick's almost black snakelike eyes. They were like a mirror of death waiting to happen.

The two holding him led him to a straight-backed wooden chair Brick moved out into the open in the one corner that had no pallets of boxes. He held out a roll of silver duct tape. Ike and Rueben taped Griff's wrists and ankles to the chair. That these items were readily handy suggested he wasn't the first to be taken to the spot. His heart was beating like a rabbit's after too much coffee. He could think of nothing he liked about the situation and was somewhere between screaming, vomiting, or perhaps both at once.

"I'll be waiting outside," Fenster said and headed out of the warehouse, probably not having the stomach for what was going to follow, which did nothing to calm or reassure Griff.

That Ike and Rueben were still pretty free about calling each other by name worried him a lot. The other guy, Brick, made Griff shiver. His dark-brown eyes had become lifeless glittering black beads. When he took off his jacket, which he'd worn even as warm as the day had been, Griff could see a slanting leather strip with a row of throwing-knife handles sticking up. The guy took one of the knives out of the sheath and walked slowly toward Griff.

"If you're trying to scare me..." Griff started.

"Then he's doing a pretty good job," Rueben said.

Griff could feel the warmth in his pants where he'd just wet himself.

"I don't think he's gonna last long, Brick," Ike said.

Oh, great, Griff thought, *now I'm the source of amusement and perhaps some side bets. I'm not going to live through this.*

Brick moved closer, letting Griff look up at him for a few moments.

"It's simple." His voice was a growl. "You tell us where the money is, and we let you live, even help us get it, and we'll split with you."

Griff doubted that very much, but if he did that he might just contrive a chance to live.

Brick reached down and squeezed Griff's upper left arm in a vise-like grip that began to act as a tourniquet, the arm turning pink then getting darker beneath the taut skin.

"You'll get ahold of your sidekick, and we work together, with us watching every step and move you make. *Capiche*?"

Griff stared up at him with what he hoped was a blank stare. But he felt himself trembling.

The hand with the knife came closer and passed in front of Griff's face, then the ever-so-sharp point descended to just touch the inside of Griff's forearm. Brick drew a line that opened into a slit not even a quarter of an inch deep. But when Brick let go of Griff's arm, blood oozed out all along the slit and dripped. The room swirled, and his head drooped as the lights went out.

He shook himself and lifted his head, realizing he had fainted. They were staring at him like a semicircle of jackals, probably looking forward to seeing him get cut again.

"I'll do it," he gasped. "I'll tell you everything."

"I thought you'd see it our way," Brick said, wiping the end of the knife on a cloth and slipping it back into its sheath.

He turned to Ike and Rueben. "Either of you want a go at thumping on him?"

"Hey, I said I'd do it!" Griff yelled.

Rueben grinned. "Let's see what he has to say first."

"Yeah," Ike agreed. "We'll see about any thumping needs doing after that."

Chapter Eighteen

Budge woke feeling sweaty, damp, and hungry, so hungry. He'd slept with the truck's windows cracked, and no one had bothered him where he'd parked as far out in the Walmart parking lot as he could. He glanced at his watch—just a little after six. The store would have just opened. He could make a *baño* run.

Once outside the truck, he locked it, stretched, and straightened his clothes the best he could. He was nowhere near as concerned about his appearance as Griff. *Poor Griff. Where is he? Is he alive?* Budge had tried to call and text but had gotten no response so far. Not good.

In the store's men's room, he splashed water on his face and drank some of it from a cupped hand. The store was just coming to life itself, with only a few customers poking about and the staff hustling around, straightening and adjusting merchandise for the day's flurry of selling.

He sauntered back to the truck, put down the tailgate, and brought out the rest of the loaf of bread and the small half-full bottle of ketchup. He began making ketchup-and-bread sandwiches, wolfing them down as fast as he could. When he ate the last bit of bread and drank the final half inch of ketchup and was still hungry, he put the empty bottle and bread wrapper in the sack and carried that all the way over to a trash container near the store's front doors. Then he went back to sit on the truck's tailgate and stare out across the parking lot, trying hard not to fret about Griff but doing just that.

A white-haired woman in a silver Volvo slowed as she passed him. The car came to a stop. The woman, as tiny and frail as the one whose house they had robbed, got out of her car and carried a box toward the truck. She opened the lid and took out two doughnuts and handed them to Budge, who wished he could be more reluctant about accepting them.

"You're just a poor starving animal of a young boy." She tilted her head up at him. "And so sad. What's bothering you?"

"I was just thinking that people sometimes need to feel needed."

"You should get yourself a dog."

"I would sure like that."

She shook her head as she went back to her car and slowly drove away.

He had eaten both doughnuts by the time her car left the lot. Budge licked sugar off his lips and suddenly felt half sick to his stomach, thinking about the woman they had robbed. He bet the woman who'd given him the doughnuts had grandkids at home, who the breakfast treats were for. *Nice old woman.* He glanced at his hand where Chico's teeth marks were still healing. *I deserved far more than that from that little dog who was just defending the house.*

He didn't know if his spirits could sink any lower. Then his burner phone rang.

"Budge, is that you?"

"Yeah, Griff. Where are you?"

"I'm not sure. I'm being held captive. They gave me back my phone to make this call."

"What can I do?"

"Nothing... for now. Look, I had to tell them about the gold."

"Did you have to?"

"They were very convincing. I had to tell them everything. I was going to get really hurt, maybe killed if I didn't."

"Are you okay?"

"I'm alive as long as I go along with them."

"What's that mean?"

"That we're all going to work together to get our hands on that treasure. All of us, them and us together."

"Really?"

"There's no choice. Not for me, anyway. You could always take off like a speckled bird if you want."

"You know I wouldn't leave you."

"Touching as that is, these are dangerous men. Are you sure?"

"I'll do what I need to do. You know that."

"Okay, if you're sure. I'll tell you where to meet up with us at dusk. They took all my money, but they can at least feed us. I imagine you're hungry."

"Very." Budge could still taste a bit of sugar on his lips, but his stomach was crying out for more. Yet his insides were bubbling in joy that Griff was alive.

"They want you to meet up with us. I asked for someplace open. There's a public boat ramp not too far from that property. Will that work for you?"

"I'll make it happen." Budge felt more reluctant than he let on. But this was Griff, after all.

"I'll see that they pick up some food for you."

"Umpf." Budge hung up. He knew he was in for a long day of watching shoppers come and go, but he had nowhere else to go nor any money in his pocket. At times like that, he grasped the feeling of the Great Depression, which he had read about, that awful feeling of not even having a dime in his pockets.

He napped when he could and walked about. The store's bathroom was the only department to get any of his business. But no one gave him the bum's rush, and a pimple-faced employee gathering up shopping carts just looked the other way when he got a glimpse of Budge's size.

Finally, it was time to go.

He had enough gas and fired up the truck, left the window open, and let the breeze sweep in across him as he started off to find the boat ramp.

As he wove through the busy afternoon rush-hour traffic until he was out onto smaller roads, he tried to think, but his fellow drivers seemed determined to go at varying speeds and do illogical things like rushing out ahead of him and going slow, all to make him pay more attention to them instead of his thoughts.

He saw a stretch of loose gravel to the right ahead and pulled over and stopped then turned off the engine. As vehicles sped or plodded past, he tried hard to weigh what he was headed toward, something he could have been doing while idling the day away in that parking lot. But his head had been in a shutdown blur of waiting mode. He hadn't even read.

Any fool who thinks he is tougher than a bullet may well find out the hard way that he was not. He had read enough action-adventure books to know that. The last time he saw these guys, they had been using automatic weapons and had been quite eager and free about it. They also could not be trusted. They almost certainly planned to kill Griff and himself once they were done using them. But to leave Griff on his own would be to say goodbye forever to him. They had been together too long for that. There had been just a subliminal hint in Griff's words that if they went along with these guys, they could figure out something along the way, like escape and maybe even make off with any gold as well. All in all, it was odds against, but he would do it, had to do it if he was to live with himself.

He turned on the engine and pulled out onto the road again. Just a few miles farther, he saw a brown sign indicating the turn for the Muleshoe Bend boat ramp and recreation area.

The sky above was dimming as the sun slowly slithered toward the horizon.

The farther he went back along the road, the more deserted the area looked. He knew the lake level had been getting lower and lower in all the hundred-degree days with no rain, but he hadn't considered what a wasteland that would make of a place where people could go to relax by the lake.

Only a few vehicles were scattered here and there. If anyone had been recreating in the area, most had headed off to their homes. He spotted the white truck parked over by the boat ramp, which was high and dry, with orange cones blocking the downward-sloping cement that no longer reached the lake. The place was perfect for the sort of meetup he expected. Big though he was, he felt himself shiver as he got closer.

He pulled up and parked twenty feet away from the four men grouped around Griff at a cement picnic table. Griff stood, and one of the men stood with him, as if expecting him to run.

Budge sighed, turned off the engine, and climbed out of the truck. *This is it. No turning back now.*

He strode over to them. As he got closer and could see Griff more clearly, he noticed his left eye was swollen half shut and he leaned with one hand on the cement table, as if his ribs hurt.

"What happened to you?"

"He let them thump on me a bit... for fun." Griff nodded toward the swarthy one with glittering black eyes. That established the leadership and the terms of employment.

Budge wished that there had been any other way out of the situation, but he hadn't been able to think of one.

"We got you some food." Griff reached to the table and held up a Sonic bag that was leaking through with a little greasy moisture.

Budge took the bag and started to sit down by Griff, but one of the men slipped between them, not wanting them to have a chance to chat and catch up, maybe to plot a way out.

"This is Ike." Griff nodded toward the one between them. "That's Rueben over there."

Rueben looked like he'd caught some thumping too and winced when he shifted on the hard seat.

"The quiet one on the end—that's Fenster. He's just a driver."

Budge took that to mean he was no real threat, but the other three sure were.

"That one"—Griff nodded toward the swarthy one—"is Brick. He's kind of running things now."

"You know their names?" Budge asked.

"Yeah, it's like that."

"Oh. I see." And he did, in a very uncomfortable way.

Griff slid a large drink container toward Budge, who was opening the bag.

It held two double cheeseburgers with bacon and an order of fries. The aroma coming up from the open bag nearly knocked him back. He opened one of the burgers, greasy in its wrapper, and began taking huge bites out of it.

"I knew you'd be pretty hungry by now," Griff said.

Budge nodded and kept eating, finishing the first double burger in record time then reaching for the fries and a packet of ketchup. He watched Griff's face, catching him flinch when he glanced toward Brick. Then he noticed a row of Steri-Strips holding a wound on his arm closed. He'd been cut as well.

Griff nodded, a little too eagerly. They'd really done a job on him. Budge hoped that Griff had nothing like Stockholm syndrome, that he was just going along so they could make an escape. He pulled the other burger out of the bag, found a napkin, and cleaned his face and fingers before opening the wrapper, regretting eating so quickly because he'd soon be out of food again.

"We'll take both trucks," Brick said, looking at Budge. "Ike and I will go with you in the red truck. Fenster will drive Rueben and your pal in the white truck."

Budge noticed the glitter on Brick's wrist. He was wearing Griff's knock-off Rolex. Griff caught the glance and looked even sadder, like he was listening to the last ticking moments of his life.

When Budge had finished scarfing down the food, he drank deeply from the drink container, which appeared to contain Dr Pepper although much of the ice had melted.

Brick stood up and waved a hand toward the trucks. The jacket he was wearing, despite it having been a hot day, swung open enough for Budge to catch a glimpse of a shoulder holster and, in it, the butt of what looked like a World War II-style Colt .45 automatic, probably loaded with a clip full of jacketed bullets.

"You have that metal detector?" Brick asked Budge.

Budge nodded.

"Then, like I said," Brick voice was a firmer growl, "I'll ride with you and Ike."

Oh, great. They were keeping Griff and him apart so that they couldn't chat.

Ike gave a quick glance toward Fenster and the limping Rueben. "Okay, I guess."

Budge took that as a hint that maybe these guys weren't always on the same team.

He slid into the driver's seat, while Ike got in the back, moving the metal detector to make room for his feet.

Brick got into the passenger side and said, "Let's go."

Budge had to turn on his lights because it had gotten so dark. He could see only a haunting part of Brick's face in the glow from the dashboard, but that did nothing to make him feel better.

He passed the lane that went back to the house on the property and turned onto the twin dirt ruts of the property where they'd parked the last time he and Griff had made an attempt to prospect for the gold.

The two trucks parked, and they all clambered out, with Budge getting the metal detector out of the back seat.

He'd barely taken a couple of steps when Brick spun and glared at him, holding a finger up to his lips.

Sure, the ground crackled like Rice Krispies and he'd stepped on a tiny twig, but Budge hardly thought he could walk on air. The others, including Griff, were staring at him, so he slowed and took far more care about where he stepped and how much noise he made. Soon, he was lagging behind the others but was far quieter than he'd been.

They had brought no flashlights, and as soon as they were in the shade of the trees, Budge could hardly see at all. He remembered he had two flashlights he and Griff had used before in the glove box, but he hadn't thought to mention them in all the hubbub and confusion of suddenly being forced to go along with the likes of Brick. By going so slowly, he was soon almost out of sight of the others, getting grabbed at by sticker bushes and nearly bumping into trees he could barely see until he almost ran into them.

Griff was way ahead, with the others. But they would have to wait for him since he had the detector. He paused to listen to hear where they'd gone but heard instead a distant barking and then the pounding of feet. Disregarding being quiet, Brick, with Fenster and the others close behind, came running toward him. *Busted again!*

Brick waved a hand in the direction of the parked trucks. Budge spun and took off running, clinging to the detector, which banged against his leg, but running as flat out fast as he could.

Chapter Nineteen

Al woke at the same time Tanner sat up in the corner and barked when the alarm went off.

"Jiminy Cricket," Al snapped, throwing off the covers. "What the hell is it with these jaspers?"

He climbed out of bed. Fergie had shot out even faster this time and was pulling on her clothes. He paused in his rush toward his clothes to admire her for a second or two as she did the opposite of a striptease by going from nude to tugging on jeans, boots, and a burgundy blouse.

When he got out into the living room, he could see enough on a lit box or two on the screen to say, "Same damned men. Half a dozen of them."

He rushed to the top of the stairway downstairs and yelled down, "Maury! Fire up the drone."

"I'm all over it," Maury yelled back.

Meat Jenkins had loaned him only two of them from the department, saying to take care of them. One of them had already bitten the dust, taken out by a thrown knife, and the man who had thrown the knife was on the screen at the moment.

Another box lit up on the television screen as Al heard the drone's buzzing roar. He speed-dialed the sheriff's department while watching the woods light up from the drone's headlight. Soon, the same fellows he could see from the other motion-detecting cameras were lit up brightly as they looked up at the drone coming toward them.

"Yep. Same damn fellows," Al said.

Fergie was slipping her Glock behind her back as she came out of the bedroom. She handed him his Sig Sauer. Tanner pushed against Al's legs, tail wagging, wanting to get in on the hunt.

The swarthy knife thrower spun and looked right up at the drone. His arm came up from inside his jacket. He held a pistol, a big automatic. The next second, the picture from the drone snapped off.

"He shot it out of the air. One shot," Fergie said. "That man is a dickens with knives or guns."

"Let's go," Al said.

"I want to go too," Bonnie said, but she stood there holding Little Al's hand.

"Stay here," Al said. "We need someone holding down the fort, and it might as well be the best shot we have."

She wasn't able to repress a smile at that, but she nodded.

As Al ran out the front door, he tried to put a foot in place to hold Tanner back, but old though the dog was, Tanner shot past and was outside, soon running along beside Fergie and Al. He barked as he ran, as delighted as though he was on a coon hunt.

In the distance, a siren was coming down the road in their direction though still half a dozen miles away.

BRICK MIGHT HAVE FELT he was pretty light on his feet and a good runner, but Budge had surged to the front of those running away. For a second or two, he wished Griff was right beside him and they could climb into the red truck and be off and away from all this. He glanced back. Griff was in the thick of the others and wasn't going to be able to keep up with Budge's pace. *Damn!*

He could hear a dog barking far away in the direction of the house.

"If that mutt gets close, I'm gonna blast it to kingdom come," Brick huffed as he ran.

"Don't you dare hurt that dog!" Budge yelled back to him.

"I'll do whatever I need or want to that damned hunk of fur. You just keep running and get that truck started and ready to go by the time we get there."

Budge at least did that, feeling flashes of heat dashing across his face as anger boiled deep inside him. But he did as told and got to the truck ahead of them and opened the door. He tossed the metal detector into the back seat, for the first time realizing he had carried it all the way, and had the truck going with passenger door and back door open. Brick and Ike scrambled in and slammed their doors, and Budge hit the gas, throwing dirt, gravel, and dried grass in a spray behind them.

Fenster and the other two were soon in the white truck and right behind them, weaving along the lane to the road. Budge turned his lights off and slowed to a stop just short of the road. Fenster caught on and did the same. The sound of the siren came their way, its blue and red lights flashing away as it whooshed by. As soon as it was out of sight, Budge lit up again and headed off in the direction the cruiser had come from.

Budge slowed down and kept right at the speed limit as soon as he felt they were far enough away from the cruisers swooping in on that property. The low response time told him those folks might have friends in law enforcement places.

Brick gave him directions as he drove, and soon he was weaving through some rough-and-tumble streets in southeast Austin, where warehouses were protected by thick chain-link fences with razor wire coiled along the tops. Brick had him stop in front of a gate. He got out and opened a large padlock. He swung the gate open and waved Budge inside. Fenster followed closely in the white truck and parked beside the red truck as Brick locked the gate and came toward them. "We're gonna have to bunk down here for the night. Tomorrow's another big day."

As they moved into the warehouse, passing between pallets stacked high with cardboard boxes, Ike peeled away to go over by Rueben, keeping Griff from coming over to Budge.

Budge figured they would keep them separated so they couldn't talk. But he sure would have liked to have a word or two with Griff. That they knew names and now knew about this warehouse did not bode well for either of them.

"Take him to the small storage room by the office, and stay with him there." Brick nodded toward Griff.

Through the office's window, Budge could see a large old-fashioned black safe in the far back corner. Ike led Griff into the small closet-sized room next to the office.

"I have a bed at home I'd like to get into," Fenster said.

"You and Rueben will stay the night and keep an eye on him. You hear me? Ike and I will be out here with this one. We have much to do tomorrow and will start early."

Fenster looked like he was about to say something. His mouth opened then closed again. He turned and went with limping Rueben as they led Griff away. Griff's head stayed lowered, and he didn't even look back at Budge.

Budge sighed. He looked around at all the boxes that surrounded them. "Is there food in any of these boxes?"

Brick pointed toward a stacked pallet where the boxes were marked MREs. He said, "Try that one." To Ike, he said, "Go bring in one of those packs of bottled water."

While Ike was away, Budge got down a box and tore open the top. He'd come across similar Meals Ready to Eat and dug eagerly through the assortment. He pulled out one marked Asian Beef Strips and passed on one marked Chili with Beans. No Texan would ever stand for beans being in chili. He found one that said Chicken Chunks he thought would be all right and handed a Beef Stew one to Ike when he came back with the water bottles.

"Can you see that Griff gets this?"

"Sure." Ike grabbed a random handful of the brown MRE bags. "The others will want a bite too. I already dropped some water off for them." He headed out of sight.

For a brief second or two, Budge contemplated jumping on Brick while just the two of them were together. But Brick was still wearing his jacket, which Budge knew concealed that Colt .45 and a handful of knives. He didn't fancy his odds against that, and Ike was soon back while Budge was digging into some chicken chunks with a small indestructible-looking spoon. Ike pulled out a meal labeled Beef Ravioli. He shrugged and opened it. Brick dug around more carefully in the open container until he found a bag marked Beef Steak w/Mushroom Gravy.

Ike finished eating first and went off then came back with three brand-new sleeping bags, still in their plastic.

"We'll bunk right here." Brick pointed to the floor.

Budge had expected nothing less. They would keep him apart from Griff. He didn't know what the morning held for them. He tossed his second empty meal aside and reached into the open crate to pull out one that said Turkey Breast w/Gravy & Potatoes. He would have a little Thanksgiving moment. Maybe that would help him sleep despite the tension of having to bunk with the likes of those two and having the looming threat of death hanging over his head. At the very least, the void in his stomach was going away.

AL'S PHONE RANG JUST as the sheriff's department cruiser closest to the house turned off its flashing lights and started up the lane toward the road. They had done all they could, made another report, and now had to go patrol the county and deal with the usual wackadoodles prowling the night highways, enraged by a domestic quarrel or more than half lit while making their way home from some pub after happy hour stretched on into the dark.

"What are you doing up at this hour?" Al asked after he glanced at the caller ID before taking the call.

"I heard you had more trespassers encroaching on your property again," Clayton said.

"There were six of them this time. The number keeps growing."

"What seems to be attracting them like moths to a flame?"

"I have no earthly idea."

"Could it be about Bonnie's cooking?"

"She does make apple dumplings and banana bread that are killer bee."

"But you don't think that's it."

"Of course not. What are you really calling about?" Al knew damn well what was putting a bee in Clayton's bonnet. But he had a right to be a little irritable and snappish himself. He had no idea why people kept trying to get onto his property again and again, while Clayton was pushing his own agenda, which might even be his own fault if what those women were saying was true.

"You know we're just a few days away from having to announce, as well as any election opponents. Please tell me you're getting closer to finding out anything that might help me."

"I wish I could. But those two women are deepwater clams when it comes to talking. I have one or two other approaches I might try, but I don't want to get your hopes up."

"My hopes are in the cellar right now. About anything positive you can dig up will only send them upward. Do keep at it. I'm counting on you."

He hung up. Al glanced at Fergie, who stood beside him. "He's not in the best of moods, and I don't blame him."

"What else can you do?"

"I've got one more trick up my sleeve. I'm going to head into the department and get a little help from our friend Meat Jenkins."

"Do you need to pick up anything sweet on your way in?"

"I don't need to. We're about a cheesecake ahead in that favor department. But I may as well swing by and get him a bucket of doughnuts."

"We're not really a healthy alternative for him, are we?"

"Try taking him a salad, and see what that gets us."

She took hold of his arm. "Come on. Let's get to bed. It'll be morning before you know it."

He heard just a little something extra in her tone that had him stepping lively as he went inside with her, locked the door, sailed past Tanner's vigorously wagging tail, and let her haul him into the bedroom.

Chapter Twenty

Budge woke to Ike nudging him in the ribs with the toe of one boot. "C'mon. Step lively. We're gonna mount a morning expedition."

Looking around for Griff and not finding him, Budge's second thought was about some kind of breakfast. He sat up and pushed his sleeping bag aside. On top of a small wooden box that acted as a table, he spotted a paper bag and a cardboard coffee container from McDonald's. They had some of the best and most dependable coffee of the fleet of fast-food companies. Someone had made an early-morning run to the nearest location. Budge still didn't have an exact idea of where he was. Watching as they had come each time and looking for landmarks, he supposed they were somewhere in southeast Austin, among a collection of older warehouses.

He opened the lid and took a sip of warmish coffee. He realized he was smacking his lips as he fished an Egg McMuffin with Canadian bacon from its paper wrapper. But he was damn hungry. He wondered for a moment if he'd lost weight during the recent days of deprivation.

Griff had often hinted that it would do him good to shed a pound or two, but he hadn't anticipated an enforced starvation diet as a captive.

Brick and Ike stood on either side of where Budge sat on the floor, crumpling the paper wrapper and putting it back in the bag. He reached for his coffee cup, which was half empty.

Griff came out to join them, flanked on either side by an irritated Fenster and Rueben, who appeared to be limping slightly less. Fenster's frown deepened as he brushed at his wrinkled clothes. A night of roughing it with the boys had probably not been his first choice. Griff, whom they seemed determined to keep away from Budge, did not even bother with his clothes although they were a complete wrinkled mess. *That's not the Griff I know.* Budge shook his head at seeing the confidence and touch of arrogance sucked out of his pal.

Brick swung a small backpack onto the box Budge had been using as a breakfast table. From it, he took out a couple of pairs of binoculars. His voice was a rough grumble. "We're gonna go have a good look around. Do our homework proper and right. *Capisce?*"

He glanced down at Budge. "You all done pigging out?"

Budge nodded although he would have willingly eaten two more of the muffin sandwiches and a couple of those little potato thingies.

He glanced toward the open lid of the box from which they had gotten those MREs and would have gladly sneaked a few if he thought he could get away with it.

Brick waved a hand. "Let's go. Fenster, you know to find a new place to park on the other side. You have a rough idea of what I said to look for. Stay way back, make as little movement as possible, and call me if you see anything."

Budge climbed back into the driver's seat, which was still warm. Brick slid into the passenger side while Ike got into the back seat, pushing aside the metal detector so that he had a place for his feet.

As they got closer to the property, a piece of land Budge was coming to know far better than he liked, Brick said, "Slow down. We've got to find a new place to go in from. That damned drone revealed the last place. It'll mean we have to walk a little farther and not let anyone spot us. But you can manage that, can't you, big guy?"

Budge grunted. He had already decided he did not care for this Brick person one little whit. The guy just oozed raw evil.

Because of established neighbors and some lots just beginning to be developed as Austin's urban sprawl penetrated that far out from the city, they had to go a little over a mile to find a place they could tuck away the red truck.

With Brick on one side and Ike on the other, Budge walked along the road until they would hear a vehicle coming. Then they all ran in a scampering clatter of hurried footsteps to get off the road and out of sight. He imagined the group with Griff was going through much the same hijinks. He would have sure liked to call Griff and have a private chat, but the two with him were keeping a close watch on him, and he suspected Brick had taken Griff's burner phone away as soon as he'd used it to call Budge.

They came at last to the lane going back to where they'd been before. Once they got all the way back, they started toward the property as quietly as they could go. When Budge made his usual loud and clumsy noises, crackling, popping, and snapping twigs, Brick stopped, turned, and glared at him, letting him know he was expendable if he continued to threaten to give them away. From then on, Budge picked each step with special care, avoiding each twig or dry-looking leaf. The smell of the woods was still of dry dirt and decaying leaves.

Brick held up a hand to stop them. "Don't anybody move from here on."

He lifted the binoculars and scanned the area ahead. "Hmm. As I thought."

He handed the binoculars to Ike. "See if you spot them."

"What am I looking for?" he asked after a moment.

"On the trees. Those cameras pick up motion and must sound some alarm. Let the lump have a look."

Ike handed the binoculars to Budge. At first, he just saw more woods, then a scrap of camouflage cloth stood out, a strap holding a small green box with a lens to a tree.

"So that's how they knew we were there," Ike said. "How do you plan on getting around those?"

"I have an idea. First, we find them all and map them out." Brick took out a small pocket notepad and drew a rectangle. He added an X. Then he got on his phone.

"You seeing anything, Fenster? Okay, then. Just mark the locations. The wind's at your back, isn't it?" When he hung up, Brick said, "That's gonna be our fire side, then."

"I hope you're not gonna set this woods on fire." Budge could picture blackened ground and wildlife creatures scurrying for their lives: deer, bunnies, and raccoons.

"No, but they may well think we did. Now, follow me as quietly as you can." He glared at Budge when he said it.

They practically tiptoed along the edge of the property, staying just out of sight and out of the range of what seemed to be motion detectors. Fearing Brick's wrath, Budge was especially watchful of stepping on anything that might crack or crackle. They were moving so silently that the sudden rustle of a lizard scampering away from them startled him. Brick didn't seem to pay the sound any mind at first, but Ike looked over at Budge with eyes that had widened for a second or two. Brick's response was different and sudden. He spun, drawing something from the inside of his jacket. His arm snapped, and a knife stuck out of the back of the small scaly lizard, pinning it to the ground, its lifeless legs still twitching as its nerves faded away.

Budge wondered for a second why the man would do that to a harmless creature. *Is he demonstrating a skill to assert his authority and ability to ruthlessly kill? Or is it to show he has no more feeling inside than the steel of the knife he pulled out of the lizard's back?*

Brick wiped the blade across leaves on the ground and put it back inside his jacket. He waved them on, and they followed, staying as close and silent as they could.

As they spotted more of the devices tied to trees along the way, Brick marked them down as little *x*'s on his rectangle in his notebook. Budge could see that Brick thought differently from how he and Griff did. He took more of a military approach that they hadn't. Maybe he could pull this whole thing off. But they still had to get away from him and his mean-as-a-snake eyes—far, far away.

He had another thought as well. The elaborate defense setup, along with the fact that someone on the property would shoot at them, gave credence to Griff's unflinching belief that there was a treasure of gold somewhere to be had, something the property owner had to defend. But he didn't know if he and Griff would have to walk away from it and be as poorly off as ever, just to escape with their lives. He would have to wait and see, but not for too long.

When they had covered their side of the property and Fenster had probably done the same on his, Brick made a quick call to him. As he hung up, he turned toward Ike and Budge. "Let's vamoose. I have enough to work with now."

Budge was happier the farther they got away from the place because they could move faster and worry less about noise. They made some of the trip on the road but, near the end, had to stay out of sight in the bramble of grabbing bushes and the cover of trees since traffic was picking up. As they emerged from the woods and he could see the red truck that had served him and Griff so well, he let out a sigh. Still, the whole blasted mess was far from over, and he only had to get a quick glance from those glittering blackish-brown eyes to know that he and Griff were standing on the edge of a cliff and were about to get shoved off the moment they were no longer of any use to this guy.

Poor Griff had not only been beaten, but he looked downright scruffy, in stark contrast to his driving effort to look dapper and sharp. The change seemed to have affected his spirit as well, sapping him. Budge wondered if he would even be up to the challenge of making an escape if the opportunity came. He would really like to have a few words with his old pal, but the guys keeping them virtual captives were conspiring to make that not easy.

As Budge drove the red truck back to the warehouse, Brick said, "Now I know what we're up against. We've got to put the kibosh on that."

"How?" Ike asked from the back seat.

Brick shared a smarmy, evil grin. "I think I know just the thing."

Chapter Twenty-One

Klive was savoring being alone in the quiet when a vehicle door slammed outside. He got up from his desk, which faced the back wall where a clock, bulletin board, and oversized calendar decorated an otherwise plain hunter-green wall. A couple of framed covers from past issues of *The Probe* hung on the wall to his left. He crossed to the windows that faced the street.

He had been fancying a cup of tea but knew he was still an hour and thirty-five minutes away from three in the afternoon, and he adhered as rigorously to tea time as the changing of the guard at Buckingham Palace. When the time neared, he would head for the corner table and turn on the electric water pot to get it boiling hot. He would fill the infuser with loose English breakfast tea from the Taylors of Harrogate tin. When ready, in its Wedgwood bone china cup and saucer, he would add a splash of milk to the tea and allow himself a plain McVitie's digestive biscuit. No Hobnobs for him—he stayed slender by choice.

His small office was located on the second floor of a building next to the classical music station and had a view out onto a side street off Lamar Boulevard. He was at a stopping place in his work for the day and felt nosy. Few people came and went in the neighborhood.

Across the street, two women were climbing out of a dark-blue Silverado. The male driver stayed in the vehicle. As the women waited for a car to pass then crossed the street, he recognized them.

"Uh-oh."

They both moved in brisk, determined strides. The thicker redheaded one, Jacqueline Frineman, glanced up at his window before he could take a step back. He didn't know if she'd seen him. She was the one who her loving friends called Wacky Jacky. The more slender blonde, Kristina Smeerna, kept her head down and her feet moving. Soon, he heard their steps coming up toward him on the narrow stairway that echoed. He waited and heard the expected tap on his door, not tentative and weak but firm and full of business.

Klive swung the door open and waved a hand toward an overlong green leather couch along one wall, a spot where he had parked his six-foot-five frame a time or two for a brief rest.

They headed across the room and plopped onto the couch, looking around briefly and probably finding the office pretty much the same as the last time they were there to talk about their story.

"Well," Jacky said, cutting to the chase, "when is our story going to publish?"

The two of them must have taken off early from their jobs to come harass him. Jacky wore a green plaid Catholic-girl skirt this time with the bobby sox and white sneakers. She had what looked like a mustard stain near the collar of her white ruffled blouse, along with another smudge of what could be spilled coffee on her sleeve. Her face flushed red as she leaned forward.

"Yeah," Kristina said. "When?" She crossed her skinny legs in jeans and leaned back. Her white blouse had a few clipped pieces of hair sticking to it where it hadn't been covered by her smock. She wore what looked like heavy-handed nightclub makeup in the middle of the day.

"I told you young ladies"—he would throw them that bone—"that a story like that takes careful fact-checking. I had a man come to me once and tell me Ike Clanton came to him in a dream and told him what really happened at the OK Corral. And he wanted the story told to the tune of 'Thunder Road.'"

"What we told you is real," Kristina said.

"Yeah." Jacky leaned forward on the couch. "We came to you in the first place because you've published exposés like ours before."

Klive towered above them and gave them what he hoped looked like an understanding smile. "I have to fact-check every story, and when the story might ruffle the feathers of a duly elected sheriff, I'm extra careful. You understand."

"We don't care how ruffled that Clayton gets. He done what he done, and the public needs to know." Kristina's face took on a rosy hue, her eyes open wide.

"Your story will get out there. Trust me," Klive said. He doubted too many other publications would even consider it without more support than they had offered. "I have people checking right now, and when I get a thumbs-up from them, I'll be full speed ahead with the story."

They turned to frown at each other then slowly stood and headed for the door.

"You'd better," Jacky said over her shoulder, then they were gone.

He let out a sigh.

His magazine could quite literally publish anything from fact to satire as long as it could squeeze a laugh or gasp from a usually jaded audience. He had once published a small insert chapbook titled *The Al Packer, Donner Party Cookbook*, with a brief preface by Sweeney Todd and a chapter on "What Will We Do with Your Clothes." A local comedy club had awarded him a Let the Farce Be with You award for that. He had the plaque still, in a drawer somewhere. The thing was, neither Al Packer nor Sweeney Todd was likely to sue him. But to mess with a sheriff of Clayton's long service was another pile of risk altogether.

He watched them cross the street and get into the dark truck, which pulled away almost as soon as the doors were closed.

Klive walked over to his desk and sat before calling a number he didn't need to look up.

"Hello, Fergie?"

"Well, howdy, Klive."

"Please tell me you have something, anything on those two women who claim they jumped Clayton's bones some thirty years ago when they were minors."

"Nothing yet, Klive, but I have hopes."

"Yes, I too have hope, but it's about all I have."

He hung up, spun his chair, and looked in the direction of the window. Those two would be headed back to their sad jobs, the memories of thirty years ago, mixed-up or real, living rent-free in their heads.

He shook his head and halfway chuckled as he said to himself, "Sometimes, life is but a joke, and you might as well have a laugh."

Chapter Twenty-Two

The warehouse had two huge exhaust fans on either end but nothing like air conditioning. The hot day outside seeped in and heated the insides to a sauna level of discomfort.

Brick had taken off his jacket and even his shoulder holster. His shirt had two big sweat patches under his arms as he took each throwing knife out of the leather sheath that held half a dozen of them in a row. He held a small carborundum hone flat on a wooden box in front of himself and honed each blade before slipping it back into the sheath.

Fenster had taken off on an errand generated by a list Brick had slipped into his hand. Ike and Rueben sat on opposite sides of the wooden box they'd used as a dining table, playing gin rummy. Griff was on the far side of the room, looking sullen and sad. Once, he tried to get up and come over to Budge, but Ike had stood, blocking his way, and pointed back to where Griff had been sitting.

As he sat back down that time, Rueben shifted uncomfortably on the little inflatable doughnut on which he sat.

"What happened to you?" Budge asked.

"One o' them assholes shot him in the butt," Ike said.

"Real bullets, then," Budge muttered. "I kinda thought so."

Budge didn't know how long they could keep him and Griff apart. Doing so foiled every chance they had to talk about any way to get out of the clutches of these men.

Sweat ran in trickles down Budge's chest, soaking into his jeans. He felt damp, uncomfortable, and hungry. Abruptly, he stood up and started across the room.

Ike stood up from the table, holding his hand of cards but staring at Budge, who was a little bigger. However, Brick was still there, honing his knives and looking up at Budge with narrowed eyes. He had several times weighed his chances against the others, figuring he could take Ike and Rueben if they squared off, and Fenster was a wheelman who he'd never seen carry a gun or act like he could fight, though he might be a surprise in a scrap or if cornered. But oh, that Brick—he was the one to watch and weigh twice in his speculations. Nevertheless, Budge kept a constant watch for the least opportunity when the odds and timing were right. Unfortunately for him, they were as vigilant at watching him and, to a lesser extent, Griff.

Instead of going toward Griff, Budge veered and went to the box of MREs. He grabbed three of them at random, tossed one over toward Griff, and carried two back to where he'd been sitting.

Ike and Rueben both looked at Brick, who shrugged.

Budge plopped back down where he'd been sitting and ripped the top off one of the meals, wondering what he'd gotten that time and not particularly caring although it might've been nice to get one of those little bars of dehydrated ice cream as a dessert.

One of the longest days of his life drifted slowly by. He finally stretched out on his sleeping bag and closed his eyes.

He woke with Ike nudging him in the side with the toe of his boot. "Wake up, sleeping ugly. It's getting on to showtime."

Brick tugging on his jacket, hot and sweaty as he was, told Budge that the swarthy guy was ready for business. His face showed that as well, with a focused meanness that would have made most people cower. It seemed to have that effect on Griff. Budge hoped he would be able to shove some of Griff's extravagant self-confidence back into him if they ever got out of their current muddle. A bath and a clean new suit of clothes wouldn't be a wrong step, he figured.

Fenster handed Brick a bag, saying, "The rest is in the white truck."

Brick wasn't one to offer effusive praise or even the smallest of thanks. Everybody did what he asked or ordered, and that was how his world was. He fished out a new roll of silver duct tape and two clip-on belt gadgets with a chain and a bottom steel bar. Brick rounded up another partially used roll of duct tape he'd probably used on Griff. He handed one of each to Ike, who knew what to do with them. He clipped the hanging chain to his belt then turned the bar to slip the roll past it. When he let go, the roll of tape hung ready at his side. Brick did the same with his.

Budge hoped they weren't thinking of trying to bind him and thump on him the way they'd done to Griff. He would go down fighting first.

Brick dumped the rest of the contents onto the table, a pack of batteries and six flashlights in their blister packs. "Get batteries into the flashlights, each of you."

Budge didn't object to having some kind of light this time instead of stumbling around in the dark. The label on the blister pack said they were focus-beam headlights. He tore the plastic off and reached for a couple of the AA batteries.

"Check your focus," Brick said. "Slide it until you have a narrow cone. We'll show the minimum amount of light that way and avoid bumping into trees and sticker bushes."

Griff was struggling to get his light out of its package.

Budge started to step toward him, but Ike stepped between, took the blister pack from Griff, and ripped it open.

Griff's glance toward Budge was sheepish, but he got the batteries loaded into his flashlight and futzed about with the focus.

Budge felt they were really headed out on a military sort of mission. Brick gave a curt wave, and they headed out to the two trucks. Budge got into the driver's side of the red truck. Dusk had gone by, and the night was getting seriously dark even though it wasn't quite seven o'clock as the two trucks pulled out. Budge glanced at the face of his cheap Timex watch, which had taken an occasional licking but kept on ticking and which hadn't been worth stealing as Griff's watch had been. He gave one quick peek to the back seat, confirming the metal detector was there.

Budge clenched the steering wheel and watched the dark shadows in thick woods go by as they went up and down hills on their way toward the lakeside lot. Before he and Griff came out to that part of Texas, he'd thought most of the state was as flat as a fritter. Central Texas's hill country, which lined the string of lakes that once flowed as the Colorado River, had burst that bubble for him. His ears were nearly popping at some of the shifts up and down in the darkness. The night seemed unusually dark, his headlights picking up pairs of reflected eyes hidden among the bushes as they swept by.

Brick had him go to the parking spot more than a mile away from the target property. As Budge got out, Ike handed him the metal detector.

"You'd best find something," Brick said, an edge of threat in every word. He slipped the strap to a pair of binoculars over his head to hang around his neck. "You remember the areas you covered and what you said the old dude swept."

Brick opened the notebook he'd used to mark where the motion-detecting security cameras were located. He handed the pad and a pen to Budge. "Mark the areas you and the other guy haven't covered."

Budge did as he was asked. Less than a third of the property remained to cover, and it was on the side where they would go in. He handed the pad back to Brick. "That's all of it."

"How long do you think a sweep of that could take?"

"Maybe an hour or two."

Brick stepped close so that his face was less than a foot from Budge's. "You have more like fifteen or twenty minutes, so be ready to get going when I say. I don't know how long our distraction can occupy their attention."

He spun and started toward the road. Budge followed, with Ike right on his heels, and he was holding an Uzi down at his side.

As soon as they got to the road and started walking along the two-lane asphalt, they had the same challenge as before, having to dash off the road and tuck away and hide. At least in the black of night, they could see headlights coming in time to start looking for a place to get out of sight.

In the quiet of the night, Budge heard rustling slithers across the dried leaves on the ground.

"Lizards?" Ike whispered.

"Maybe." Brick spoke out loud.

Budge had heard that in super-hot weather, as they had been experiencing, rattlesnakes came out to hunt from dusk to dawn, a fact that didn't make him welcome having to dash into the woods from time to time.

The edges of the road were far from perfect, with occasional patches missing, as if something big had taken a bite from the asphalt here and there. In the dark, Budge had a hard time seeing them. He nearly tripped when his toe caught on the edge of one as they hurried off the road to cower in a patch of sumac beside the trunk of a large live oak.

Three pickup trucks closely spaced together whooshed past from one direction while a single sedan passed from the other.

They got back onto the road as the lights and sounds faded away. Brick broke into a near trot so that they wouldn't have to keep finding hiding places.

Brick led them off the road when they were near enough to ease in for a glimpse at the property.

Budge knew Brick had spotted some motion-detecting cameras acting as a defense mechanism. But he didn't know how they were going to be able to do anything about that.

When they were close enough to the property, Brick stopped. "Don't use your lights yet. Ike, you know what to do."

Budge stood beside Brick, waiting. For a second or two, he weighed the odds of swinging the metal detector as hard as he could at the back of Brick's head.

But Brick didn't turn his back to Budge but kept staring at him as if sharing some of the same thoughts. One hand was inside his jacket as well, probably touching a knife or gun. Budge let wisdom prevail and stayed still where he was.

Ike had eased far off to their left and disappeared into the thick woods.

"What's he going to do?" Budge asked.

Brick had the binoculars up but shook his head. "Too dark to see a damned thing." He turned toward Budge. "He'll ease up behind the tree and slip a strip of tape to cover the lens and motion detector in one quick swoop. If he's careful and quick, it shouldn't set off any alarm. We'll cover this side enough for you to do some detecting."

Ike came out of the woods, walking toward them. "That one's done."

Budge glanced at his watch and figured Ike had taken twenty-five minutes to half an hour to do one camera. With three more do on this side, it was going to take him quite a while to clear the area enough to detect all of it. But he might be able to get started once a couple of the cameras were disabled. Still, a long night loomed ahead.

"Is Fenster doing the same on the other side?" Budge figured Rueben would be the one keeping an eye on Griff.

"No. I've something a little different for that side." He turned to Ike. "Go do the next one. I'll get this lump started on some detecting."

Budge could have objected to being called a lump, but he was still biding his time, looking for just one really good opportunity.

With Brick pressing closely behind him, Budge slipped on the headset, turned on the detector, and moved forward with side-to-side sweeps. He had his hands full with keeping a narrow cone of light from his flashlight on the ground to see where he was going and not bonk into a tree or a thorny bush.

He kept the volume turned down low so that he doubted if Brick heard any of the mild peeps of what were probably soda can pop tops. A louder signal made him stop, and Brick nearly ran into him although he had the narrow beam of his flashlight poking around at the ground they passed.

Budge took the heavy-duty plastic hand trowel he kept taped to the side of the detector and bent to dig, coming at last to find the target was only the broken blade of a penknife. He skipped some more small pips after that. A pile of gold bullion like they sought would send a target signal so loud that he would probably have to yank off the headset.

The woods around them seemed dark and mysterious as he focused on the thread of light he cast on the ground. Brick had been right about one thing. Cutting off the vision from the motion-detecting cameras did give him time to cover the ground he hadn't had a chance to check yet. But not finding anything while less and less area remained to cover was sending a niggle of doubt about whether there was any treasure to find. Someone else might have beaten them to it. Worse, if they did find a pile of gold, that would just mean Brick would probably kill him and Griff, taking the treasure for himself.

Thinking about it like that rather took any thrill of discovery away from his effort. But a glance back at Brick's narrowed eyes and the one hand inside his jacket where he could get to a gun or knives kept Budge going as he covered as much of the remaining ground as he could in the brief time they had.

Chapter Twenty-Three

Al and Fergie sat at the dining table, each holding a book with an empty coffee mug on the table. Since the television was dedicated to the security system Dirty Fingernails Huff and Meat Jenkins had set up for them, they had both gravitated to the bookshelves and were reading. As former detectives, he had picked out a novel featuring Maigret, active on the streets of Paris, while Fergie was reading one of the tales featuring Inspector Porfiry Rostnikov set in Russia and written by Stuart Kaminsky. He was off to France while she roamed the streets of Moscow, and outside in the dark, the hill country of Central Texas supposedly slept quietly.

Two bookshelves in the living room and another in the master bedroom held the books Al had intended to read in the quiet of living out his retirement alone with no reason for the world to disturb him. But, as he sometimes put it, look how things had turned out.

Maury sat on the couch and looked perfectly happy to be just holding Little Al. "I can't believe the direction my life has taken," he said, giving the giggling boy a hug.

Al couldn't either since Maury had been quite the horndog of a woman chaser before Bonnie tamed him.

The television gave the occasional twitch, as their techie friends had said it would, at gusts of wind and such, but no alarms had sounded so far that evening, not even a coyote, possum, or raccoon tripping one of the motion-sensing alarms.

Bonnie came in the front door, her round shape pressing against the jeans and checked blouse she wore. Her curly blond hair had been tousled by the wind. She ran the fingers on one hand through it. "It's just me."

Tanner rose from where he was curled up at Al's feet and trotted over to greet her.

She carried the 30-06 rifle with scope. "Nothing was doing up toward the front. I took only a quick eyeball around since we should be okay if those cameras are working. Haven't heard anything, have you?"

"Not a creature is stirring, not even a mouse," Fergie said.

Bonnie nodded. "So I went down and took a brief scout by the lake. Nothing doing there either. It's kind of nice to be having a quiet night for a change, but it creeps me out a little."

"We've all been on edge lately," Fergie said. "It's a blessing to have nothing going on for a change."

Bonnie carried the rifle as she crossed over to Al and Fergie's bedroom to put the weapon away in the gun safe.

When she came back out of the bedroom, she went over to the stove and checked on the pot of coffee there. She opened the fridge's freezer side and took a long, careful look in there then started to take all the cans and other food containers out of the pantry and spread the contents across the countertops.

"What are you doing?" Maury asked while Little Al grabbed at his nose and he dodged in keep-away.

"I'm taking a little inventory to see what we have to get by. We haven't had much of any kind of chance to do regular shopping since that would leave us shorthanded on our watches." She shook her head, and her blond curls bounced about. "We've got canned spinach, green beans, and peas that can stand in for salad, as well as some veggies in the freezer. Though we're about out of onions. There are two cans of pears and three of sliced peaches. That'll take the place of fresh fruit. There's flour, sugar, and plenty of dried beans."

"Please, no more beans," Fergie said.

"I could make some pasta from scratch, but we're about out of eggs."

"We'll make it somehow," Al said. "We always have."

"Sure we will." Bonnie started putting everything back into place. When she was done, she went right to the couch to sit with her thigh pressing against Maury as she reached for Little Al to hug him close.

"It sure is nice," she said, "that nothing's going on for a change."

"The quiet bothers me more than it should," Al said. "We've been through something like this before, but this time, what's different is that there are more of them each time, and whoever is leading them might well be clever and dangerous. And what's worse is we don't know what's motivating them."

Al tilted his head, hearing something ticking or dripping. He glanced toward the kitchen sink a few feet away and saw nothing there. A coffee pot half full sat warming on the stove. He'd meant to pour that into the thermos. He decided to do it later as he lifted his book and was back at once to looking down at the pavement of a street running along the Bois de Boulogne, where Maigret, puffing on his pipe, examined a body that had been dumped from a car that must have barely paused before going on its way.

RUEBEN WAS STILL LIMPING. But he carried his .357 Ruger in one hand down at his side where he could readily swing it up and open fire. So he acted as a guard. Fenster made Griff carry one of the small grills from the back of the truck. Rueben's role was to ensure that Griff didn't try to cut out and take off running.

"What are these for?" Griff asked.

Fenster carried another grill. Griff had seen four of them in the back of the truck. Fenster had bought them somewhere they were already assembled. Another good-sized cardboard box was in the truck bed, but Griff hadn't gotten a good look at it.

"Don't you worry about it," Fenter said. "We're sort of the backup plan. We run the least risk. At the first sign of any kind of trouble, we're out of here faster than a toupee in a hurricane."

"Stay back, and don't risk making any movement a motion detector might pick up." Fenster placed one grill a few feet behind a thick tree. He directed Griff to carry the other grill farther along until they could position it behind another tree.

They all went back to the truck, where Fenster and Griff picked up the other two small grills. "Are you up to carrying that box of flares?" Fenster asked Rueben.

"I'll manage." Rueben shoved the pistol he held inside his belt at the front and picked up the box.

For a split second, Griff did some math, calculating his chances of getting away if he ran. But Rueben could always drop the box and shoot Griff. Plus, taking off would leave Budge behind to be slaughtered.

Rueben moved slowly but kept up with them. "How's this work?"

"If I get a signal from Brick, we set off flares and put them in the grills. To the security cameras, which are just far enough away, it'll look like the woods are on fire. But we can still move around fine to get away. It's a first-class distraction."

Griff knew that Budge had been worried about setting the woods on fire. His concern was as much for the forest creatures. Griff's own concern had been that a fire would make the land around the house barren and black with no place to hide as they continued their search for the gold.

"Oh, cripes!" Fenster yelled and dropped the grill he held, making a loud clatter. He backed away from where he'd been. "Damnation!"

"What's the matter?" Rueben asked.

"I've been bitten by a rattlesnake. I heard its rattle too late."

Griff had heard from Budge, something he'd read in a book, that a rattlesnake can't hear its own rattle. But he doubted the little factoid would interest Fenster at the moment.

"Damn. Damn. Damn. We've got to get the hell out of here, and fast. Ow."

Chapter Twenty-Four

Fenster was gripping his leg, looking at them with the pleading eyes of a dying man. Griff hoped no one suggested sucking the poison out. Besides that being a disproven technique, it was nothing he was willing to do, even at gunpoint. A tourniquet was a bad idea as well. The best thing was to stay calm, always a challenge in such a moment, and seek professional help.

"I need to get to a doctor, pronto."

"There's Doc Samuels," Rueben said. "He's the one who patched me when I got shot in the... when I was wounded."

They abandoned what they'd been carrying, dropping it quietly to the ground, and moved back to the white truck as fast as they dared go.

"You'd better drive, Rueben." Fenster took the key they found tucked behind one visor and handed it over. He got carefully into the back seat, holding one leg up with both hands. "Ow. Ow. Ow."

In the passenger seat, Griff put his seat belt in place.

"Just go," Fenster said. He took out his cell phone and punched a number. "We had to abort," he said when he got an answer. "I've been snakebit."

Griff supposed Brick had shifted to a frowning scowl.

"I can't help it. I need to get medical help, as quickly as I can. This isn't worth dying over. The stuff is where you wanted it." He listened for a moment then answered, "No, I can't go back and get it. We're already moving."

He hung up. That would probably make Brick angry, but Griff doubted that Fenster gave a big whoop about that at the moment. Every story he'd ever heard about rattlesnake bites was probably racing through his head, along with graphic video flashes of those bitten, especially those maimed or dead as a consequence. Griff knew that was how his own head would be dealing with the moment.

By the time Rueben pulled the truck up to the curb in front of a small brick house set thirty or forty feet back from the street, Fenster sounded like he was hyperventilating in the back seat. He still clasped his leg like it might fall off. Rueben came around so that Fenster could lean on him, and Fenster waved a hand for Griff to get closer as well.

Hopping on one leg with an arm around the other two, Fenster made it to the front door.

Griff noticed a white wooden post that had once held a sign. He had gathered the doctor no longer had an active practice but could be trusted to discreetly handle gunshot wounds.

Rueben, who had wisely left his Ruger in the truck, pushed the doorbell until the front door was finally opened by a small man with frizzled white hair that swept down into bushy sideburns and a thick mustache.

"What?" The word slurred as he spoke, and the man's eyes were somewhat bloodshot and rummy.

Griff had an immediate hunch why Doc Samuels was no longer practicing.

"Rattlesnake bite," Fenster said. "You've got to help me."

"Come inside. I'll take a look. How long has it been?"

"A little over an hour," Fenster said. "We got here as quickly as we could."

"Get those pants off. Are you in a lot of pain?"

Fenster looked like he was on the edge of going into shock as he kicked off his shoes, climbed out of his pants, and lay back on what looked like a coffee table covered in a white sheet. Griff could see the two tiny bleeding holes on Fenster's leg.

Rueben stepped closer to lean down and take a good look. Griff realized he was near a door and could probably get a step or two on them.

With the doc occupied with Fenster, only the limping Rueben could give chase. For the first time since he'd been held captive, Griff had a better than even chance of getting away, having known the whole time that he would probably be killed if he didn't get away somehow. He was half a step away from taking off in a blur until he thought of Budge, who had come in when he didn't have to so he could maybe help Griff. It wouldn't be fair to him for Griff to take a flyer and leave him hanging. He would have to wait and see if a chance for them both to get clear didn't come up. He let out a small sigh. Rueben looked up at him.

The doctor held the end of his stethoscope to Fenster's chest. "Your heart is beating like a masturbating bunny."

"I've just been bitten by a snake. Could you please hurry?"

The doctor reached for a half-full bottle of Seagram's gin that happened to be sitting on a shelf, poured some on a cotton swab, and swept that across the wound.

"Ow. Ow. Ow."

Samuels bent closer to look at the wound then pushed on it with a finger.

"Ow. Ow. Ow."

"How's that feel?" the doctor asked.

"What does the word 'ow' convey to you?"

Samuels held up a tongue depressor, and Fenster opened his mouth. The doc looked inside and shook his head.

"What?" Fenster's voice went up an octave.

"You should pat yourself on the back for being one of the luckiest men alive today."

"Lucky?" Fenster was up to a near shout. "How the hell am I lucky?"

"Well, for one, I don't have any antivenom, and if I could get some, the price would be around three thousand dollars a vial, and you'd need four to six vials for an initial dose. At a hospital, the process could run as much as fifty to seventy-five thousand dollars."

"How am I lucky?" Fenster repeated.

"Because you're not in extreme pain, and I mean it would be extreme. There's no excessive bleeding or swelling in the mouth or throat that would make it hard for you to breathe. Nor are you lightheaded or drooling or going into shock."

"How is all that good?"

"It means you probably had a 'dry bite.' About a third of the time, a rattlesnake bite contains no venom at all. A dry bite."

"Really?" Fenster felt about himself with his hands and looked for a darker line moving up his leg. He had none. "You mean I'm going to live?"

"Looks like it," Samuels said, putting away his things.

Fenster reached for his pants. "Should I take anything for it?"

"Maybe a couple of aspirins, unless you'd rather a glass of gin."

Fenster shook his head.

"I'll bill Moog," the doctor said. "Go home, and get some rest. You've had a shock."

As they left the house, heading for the truck, Fenster muttered, "Home. I wish. We'll be stuck another night in that damn warehouse."

Griff wasn't looking forward to that either. But he was still alive and could cling to a tiny ray of limping hope that he and Budge could break clear of this bunch before it was too late.

BUDGE HAD THE METAL detector turned on, and Ike had shoved his pistol inside his belt and was going along beside him, shining a fine point of light ahead so that he could see where he was sweeping the search coil back and forth. Brick stayed right behind them.

He was ignoring the pips and pops of targets too small to matter, probably more damn pop tops and the like. He paused at one spot to dig up what turned out to be the rusty end of a broken garden trowel.

Budge knew if they came across a stash of gold the size they were talking about, an alarm was going to go off on the target like Fort Knox being robbed at the end of the world.

Brick reached out and tapped him when a phone call came in.

Budge listened to his half of the conversation, but when Brick hung up the phone, he asked, "What's going on?"

"Damn fool got himself bit by a rattlesnake."

"Griff?"

"No. Fenster."

Budge let out a long breath.

"There are rattlesnakes out here?" Ike's voice was louder than it should have been.

"Let's wrap up for now. We'll have to try again tomorrow. No sense risking this without our backup plan being in place. Everything might come right at us." Brick gave a curt wave.

Budge was relieved to turn off the detector and follow as they made their way quickly back to the red truck.

Brick had Budge drive around to the other side, where Fenster had driven in.

"Come on. We've got to pick up some stuff," Brick said. "Can't just leave it out here."

"Isn't this where a rattlesnake bit Fenster?" Ike asked.

"Yeah, but it's probably long gone. C'mon."

"Probably," Ike muttered. But he followed along with his light darting about on the ground until they came to where some small outdoor grills and a cardboard box sat.

Brick held up a hand and whispered, "We should be just outside the range of the motion detectors, but be slow and careful about any movement all the same, and turn off those lights."

Ike snatched up a couple of grills as though a rattler was coiled under them, and Brick took another two. Budge picked up the cardboard box that, even in the dim light, he could see contained flares when he slid it into the back of the truck.

"Now, let's get the hell out of here," Brick said. "Tomorrow's another day. I was hoping to be done with all this crap tonight."

He hadn't mentioned a thing about Fenster, whether he was going to be all right. But Budge thought about that all the way back to the warehouse. He didn't wish any special harm to come to Fenster, but that would mean one less of them if a chance came up for Griff and him to get away.

Chapter Twenty-Five

On their way back to the warehouse to meet the others, Fenster swung into the parking lot of an Academy sporting goods store. They had fifteen minutes to go before the store closed at nine.

With Rueben limping along behind Griff, they headed for the shoe department once they were inside. Fenster knew what he was after. He pulled a box of boots down and sat on a bench to try them on. The box said they were Snake Shield Armor boots. They looked like regular brown leather boots to Griff, with a brown camouflage pattern on the sides and front. They had thick waterproof soles.

"I should get some too," Rueben said and nosed around until he found his size. As he plopped down onto the bench and started taking a boot out to try, Griff just stood there, aware they were taking preventative measures against snakes while he got none, another indication that he was marked to die before the adventure was over.

"Who's gonna pay for these?" Rueben asked.

"Moog Palance can, or Semion Kashov for all that. He seems to have taken over the operation."

They were using way too many names to let Griff believe he was ever going to survive. He thought of taking off at a run while they both had a boot halfway on, but he doubted he could outrun them even in those conditions. His ribs still ached from being at the very least cracked and maybe broken. The swelling of his left eye had gone down, but he had still looked pretty hideous the last time he caught a look at himself in a mirror. The Steri-Strips covering the wound on the inside of his left forearm added to his faintly Frankenstein look, and one knee of his corduroy pants was ripped open. He looked like someone who slept in the streets and had fallen down some stairs or a fire escape while doing so.

Fenster and Rueben checked out, with Griff between them. The store closed and locked its doors as they left. Once outside, they herded Griff to the red truck and were soon headed back to the warehouse.

BUDGE THOUGHT GRIFF was starting to look like the last chapter of "What's the Use" when he came back into the warehouse with the other two.

"Get what rest you can," Brick told them. "We'll try again tomorrow."

Budge tried to catch Griff's eye as Rueben eased him down into a far corner and tossed him a sleeping bag, treating him like he was some dog they'd found on the street.

Griff's head was down, but occasionally he sneaked a side-eye look around. That was encouraging and told Budge that Griff was poised to scoot like greased lightning if they got half a chance. He would have a better chance of getting free since Rueben was slowed by his wound and Fenster wasn't one of the thugs, just a driver.

When they talked about what they would do when they found the gold, Griff had shared high-blown thoughts about expensive cars, travel, and the kind of clothes he deserved to wear, including a genuine Rolex like his fake one sparkling on Brick's wrist.

Budge had wanted a quiet little home just big enough to store lots of books, maybe a nice reading chair too.

He rose and went over to the open box of MREs. He took out a couple for himself and two more for Griff. No one said a thing. Budge tossed the two for Griff over to him.

Brick shook his head, but they all stayed in sulky silence. His eyes narrowed only a bit. He took out one of his knives and his hone and began the fingernails-on-a-chalkboard task of sharpening the blade once again, though they could hardly need it. Perhaps it was just to keep his hands busy instead of poking a knife into one of them.

Budge shrugged and sat with his back to the warehouse wall. He tore the top off the meal in the pouch he held, not even caring what it held. He was starting to like the damned things, but that could be because he felt he and Griff were being half starved to death.

He wolfed down the contents of both bags as quickly as he could, tossed the empty bags on the floor, wrapped the sleeping bag around himself, and turned his face to the wall. *Tomorrow is another day, Scarlett,* he thought. Maybe some glimmer of an opportunity to escape with their lives might present itself.

Chapter Twenty-Six

Al drove the familiar route to the sheriff's department, a big sprawling complex of buildings including a jail and garages. He felt a twinge that he no longer worked there as he had for so many years. But he did enjoy sleeping in when he wanted and taking the boat out to go fishing on workdays.

He parked in a lot for visitors, which seemed only fair, and walked across to a small annex building.

As they had agreed, Meat Jenkins stood just outside the door, and as Al approached, Meat unlocked the door with a key. His eyes were fixed on the bag dangling from Al's hand.

"Whatcha got there?" Meat, as his nickname suggested, was stocky and short. Some in the department said he looked like he'd met the three little pigs and had eaten them all. His black hair was neatly part-ed, and he had trimmed his full, bushy black beard recently. He wore jeans and a pale-green button-down shirt with no tie. He often stated that techies don't wear ties.

"I swung by that happy Latino *panadería* bakery you like and got you some *conchas*. I didn't know if you preferred chocolate or vanilla, so I got some of both. The whole place smelled of cinnamon bread."

"Aw man." Meat reached for the bag and yanked out one with a crusty, crackled round yellow top, from the cookie dough being baked on top of the cinnamon bread.

No one else was in the small building at the moment. File cabinets and piled boxes of stored records lined the walls. Small desks for recordkeeping and sorting sat between shelves filled with old logbooks and dusty volumes.

"You gonna tell me what you're looking for?" Meat asked, chewing as he spoke.

"I just need to look at some of the old logs. Bit of a homework project." Al knew Clayton hadn't told anyone in the department about his concerns.

Meat shrugged and led the way to a back corner while brushing crumbs from his thick black beard. He waved a hand toward a microfiche machine and pulled a three-legged waist-high stool over to it. "Most of the records for the time frame that interests you were converted into this format before the computer era was ushered in. Good luck to you. I've got to head back to my office and look busy."

Meat Jenkins gave a small wave and waddled off toward the door while Al slid open a drawer and started looking at box after box of microfiche film. Of course they weren't in any chronological order. That would have made it too easy. Someone had juggled them around until they were a higgledy-piggledy mess.

Al started going drawer by drawer, searching. Almost an hour into the hunt, he finally stumbled across the right box of film, at least according to the dates on it. He seemed to remember that the department used to have a deputy or two with severe OCD. Why they weren't assigned to organize the room he was in was beyond him.

The room was so deathly still he could hear the clock high on the far wall ticking. He put the film in the machine and turned and turned as log pages flew by in a blur. Of all the kinds of detective work he'd ever done, the sort he was doing at that moment was his least favorite. But it had to be done, and he couldn't assign anyone else to the task. He bet Maury would have enjoyed a paper chase.

At last, he neared the date, and as soon as he scrolled the pages up to June 7, he rocked back on the creaky stool. Where that page was supposed to be, he could see only a page-long burn. He seemed to recall that if someone left a page in place too long, the bulb illuminating it might just begin to burn it, and they would have to scroll on. This seared blot, to his untrained eye, looked like it had been done on purpose. He didn't like where his thoughts were whirling to right away. But he wondered if Clayton himself had done the eradication of the only evidence of what might prove one way or the other what happened way back then.

He tugged out his phone and called his pal Meat Jenkins.

When he answered, Al asked, "Can just anyone come into this area? Is there a sign-in sheet?"

"You'd need a key," he said, "and did you sign in?"

"No."

"I rest my case."

"Well, someone seems to have burned away the records for the date I was after. Is there another way?"

"I'll come right over. I can get away for a bit as long as no IT disasters crop up."

"Like the one I'm having here."

"I'm on my way." Meat hung up.

A few minutes later, Al heard the door open and close. Meat came bustling over to where Al still sat on the stool. He saw the burned-out area.

"That's no accident," he said. He still had a few crumbs in his beard. Al suspected the *conchas* he'd brought for Meat were history.

"I don't think so either." Al didn't want to mention Clayton.

"There might be another way. Some of this back stuff was getting transferred over to computer records, but it got to be too time-consuming and expensive, more than the effort was worth. But we can see if they got as far as what you're after."

He went over to a computer, sat down in a rolling office chair that complained a little as he settled into it, and turned the PC on. Al moved closer to look over his shoulder.

Meat's chubby fingers danced in a flurry across the keyboard. After a moment or two, he said, "I think you may be in luck here, Al."

Al watched the cursor slide along a column of files and finally click on one.

"Well, I'll be a monkey's second cousin," Meat gasped.

Al stared at the blank screen.

"It's gone from here too," Meat said, too rapt in the moment to note he was belaboring the obvious.

"Oh man. I think that sinks my ship," Al said.

Meat tilted his head. He turned to look at Al. "There is one more excruciating way, a way I wouldn't wish on an enemy."

"But you'll make an exception for me?"

"Follow me."

He rose and was glad Meat hadn't said, "Walk this way," since he moved in a brisk waddle.

He had to take out another key to unlock what looked like a closet door. The insides, once he swung the door open, weren't much bigger than a good-sized walk-in closet. Metal shelves taller than Al's head formed narrow aisles.

"They were going to throw these out. Maybe burn them or something. But since this room was empty at the time, they bunged them all in here."

"What are they?" Al asked.

"The original department logbooks. Since they were moved here in haste from the other building so guys like you could have more guns and such handy back in the day, they weren't kept in any order, just put on the shelves to stay here untouched for all time."

"Except for now," Al said. "Where do I start?"

"Wherever you feel lucky," Meat said. "Like I said, this is serendipity with spurs on in here."

"Holy crap on a biscuit." Al looked at the rows and rows of logbooks. "I may be here all day. I might even have to call out for food."

"I can tell you where you can get a couple of quite tasty pizzas."

"A couple? Why two?"

"You wouldn't forget your starving friend, would you?"

How Meat could say that when he still had crumbs from his last Al-sponsored binge speckled in his beard was beyond Al. He shook his head.

Meat headed for the annex door. "Give me a call when the pizzas get here," he called back over his shoulder.

Al sure didn't plan on being all day at the task, but he wouldn't know until he got started. He walked to the end of one row of metal shelves and starting looking at the spines of the logs. At least most had the dates covered on the spine. But in some cases, that had worn or fallen off, and he had to pull the log off the shelf and look for a date. *Oh man,* he thought, *this is going to be a needle in a haystack of an all-day sucker.*

He would pull an unmarked volume out, glance at the date, and slide it back onto the shelf. The ones with dates on the spines needed only a glance. But he could find no chronological order at all. Going as fast as he could, he realized how long it was taking him to scan a single shelf, and there were many, many shelves. He sighed.

The vast number of days and lives affected by the countess incidents that made up the day-after-day life of sheriff's deputies felt overwhelming when looked at in review. The thirty-plus years of his own life as a deputy and then detective were also chronicled in bits and snippets in the logs, as well as vacations, appearances, and the humdrum of an occasional sick day.

Two and a half hours after he started, he pulled out a volume, opened it, and gasped. "Oh my God. This is it."

He leafed through the pages and finally got to June 7. Whoever had gotten to the records to remove them from the microfiche and computer records had probably not known about that original copy of the log. He breathed a huge sigh of relief that the person doing the tampering wasn't Clayton. The page he was looking at for the seventh showed that Clayton was far away at a law enforcement conference in Chicago but that Nelson Jeremiah was signed out for the weekend to represent the department at the Weeping Willow Camp. He had the evidence Clayton needed. He carried the log over to a copy machine and made a couple of copies, folded them, and put them in his pocket. Clayton didn't want anyone in the department to know about the situation, so Al figured he would call him when he got home.

When he put that log volume back, he slipped it behind others and put the shelves back into some order, wiping dust away from as many shelves as he could so that no one could tell where he had stopped his search.

"I'm done here," he told Meat Jenkins when he got him on the phone.

"You didn't even have any lunch."

"I will so do when I get home. Bonnie has a big pot of beans waiting, and they're in their second day, just getting really good."

"Aw, man. Now you've made me hungry again."

"Life's a battle," Al said. "Thanks for your help."

"You never said what you were looking for."

"Nope. I guess I didn't."

"But you found it?"

"Yep. I finally did."

"Not gonna tell me, right?"

"You've got it. Probably later. You'd better lock up the annex after I leave."

When he was just about to leave the small building, a cardboard box on a shelf by the door caught his eye. Inside, it was piled half full of old worn handcuffs, some tarnished and a few showing what looked like chips off the nickel coating and even rust. He counted out half a dozen. That was how many people he'd seen at the latest incursion. He and Fergie always had handcuff keys on their key rings. As Fergie put it, "You never know." He would clear borrowing them with Clayton later, but he doubted if he or anyone else gave so much as a big whoop.

On the way home, he swung into an HEB grocery and picked up some much-needed supplies. Bonnie had said to be sure to get a cabbage, that she could always do something with that and even had a can of corned beef. He hoped she wasn't going to cook corned beef and cabbage on a hundred-plus-degree day, but he got a cabbage all the same.

He also got plenty of eggs, bacon, some arugula, tomatoes, onions, lemons, apples, bananas, and a loaf of rye bread. The load was small enough that he could carry it to the truck, but those items were going to bring great joy back at their besieged property.

As he got into his truck to drive home, Al felt the ripping buzz he'd often experienced when solving a case in his detective days. Clayton would surely be pleased. But for the moment, he needed to get home. Whatever the hell was going on there felt far from over despite the fact that none of it made any sense at all to him yet.

The rush hour hadn't set in yet, but the day's heat had. Still, Al drove back toward his place with the two-sixty air conditioning going, something that went back to the days of older trucks—both windows open and going sixty miles per hour. The wind swept across his extended elbow and tugged at his hair. He had the radio turned up so Tom Waits's throaty growl could serenade him and help him celebrate on the way home.

Chapter Twenty-Seven

Budge's eyes snapped open, taking in a close-up view of the warehouse wall. His blanket was still pulled up close around his neck. He felt a hand at his backside, trying to wriggle into his pocket and take his wallet.

He was quite a bit faster than most people reckoned. He spun, throwing off the sleeping bag, and grabbing the wrist of the hand. Budge squeezed hard as he twisted.

Ike stood there, trying to pull back from where he was stopped, his eyes getting wide as he screamed. "Hey! Hey! That's my trigger hand."

"Let go of his hand!" Brick had his gun out and pointed at Budge.

To Budge, the end of the barrel looked as big as the open top of a bushel basket at that moment. He let go, and Ike drew his hand back and cradled it in his other hand.

"Damn big oaf might've broken my shooting hand." His voice was still an octave higher than usual. His face puckered from the pain.

"You can steal my wallet when I'm dead," Budge said.

"Won't be all that long," Ike muttered. He crossed the room, still holding his right hand in his left.

Not really the most motivational halftime pep talk, Budge figured as he rose and folded his sleeping bag.

"Best you all get up and shake off the cobwebs. It's starting to get dark outside, and we're gonna make another go of it." Brick slid his gun back inside his jacket. He glowered at them, especially Budge.

Griff stood against the far wall with his sleeping bag wrapped around his shoulders. His face showed the same underwhelmed realization that their lives mattered very little to these men and in only a short while, they would face being rubbed out like a cigarette butt in an ashtray.

Fenster came into the warehouse from outside, looking refreshed, like he'd slipped away and slept in a real bed while they'd all had to make do with the warehouse floor. "It's starting to get dark outside. You'd best all get ready to rock and roll. I sure as hell hope this is our last night at the godforsaken place."

"What're you grousing about? You and Rueben got them snake boots on." Ike was flexing the fingers of his right hand while glaring at Budge. He handed over his Uzi to Rueben and took the .357 Ruger with a six-inch matte rib barrel since he could at least use it with his left hand. He tried switching it over to his right hand, shook his head, and switched it back to his left. He started to raise the barrel toward Budge. Brick gave a tiny half shake of his head, and Ike stopped.

He flexed the fingers of his right hand and glared at Budge. "You're one dead man walking," he muttered.

The sky was dimming rapidly by the time they went out to the trucks. The grills and box of flares were still in the back of the red truck. Brick had them move those over to the bed of the stolen white truck.

Ike had his roll of duct tape hanging from his belt.

"You gonna be okay with what you gotta do?" Brick asked him.

"I'll be just fine," Ike said, still flexing his hand. "Stupid oaf."

He was the kind of lunkhead who couldn't take credit for the fact that he'd been the one trying to rob Budge. A lot of that sort were out in the world.

Budge slid into the driver's side while Brick got into the passenger seat. Ike sat in the back seat. It would be easy for Ike to fire a shot into Budge's head from behind. But he wouldn't risk causing them to crash, and they still had some good to squeeze out of Budge and Griff before they could dispose of them. But Budge was hyperaware that the old clock was ticking away on his existence unless he thought of something.

Brick was giving Budge a bit of side-eye now and then too. Budge knew he was being considered something of a loose cannon at the moment, so he kept his mouth closed as he drove, the sky getting darker around them all the time.

As they neared the property, the sky was nearly dark enough for them to get right to their tasks. He could still make out and read a Burn Ban sign, so he knew Brick would wait a few more ticks before risking any movement.

Before he could turn in where they had gone in before, Budge spotted a square silver vehicle coming their way in the other lane that he knew right away had to be a sheriff's department SUV cruiser. He kept going right past their turn, staying just at the speed limit. Fenster, in the truck a few lengths behind them, did the same thing.

The tension in his truck was palpable. Budge could feel both Ike and Brick glaring at him as he followed their directions and drove. It was dark and nasty, and an element of threat from cops had been added briefly to the mix, all just what he needed. He could feel their eyes burning into him when they looked his way, probably picturing him twitching as they pulled triggers and watched his last breath or two gasp away.

A mile or two and a couple of curves later, Budge turned left into a drive, backed out again, and started back the way they needed to go. Fenster made a U-turn behind, and they were all headed back the way they needed to go. The sky was quite black by then, so instead of waiting, they could get right at their chores.

Fenster turned in where they could work their way onto the property from the far side. Budge went past the property's drive and turned in where they would have a hike but could come in from the side where he still needed to use the detector. He parked and got out of the truck. The sky was dark enough that they could get right to it as soon as they got onto the property after Ike disabled the cameras. As he turned on his penlight to check his gear, making sure the detector had enough juice and the digging trowel was still clipped in place along the shaft, he caught a glimpse of Ike's eyes. They had gone the same lifeless black stone of Brick's—the eyes of a killer looking at someone already dead walking.

He was going to have to be on the lookout for more than rattlesnakes while they were out in the woods.

Only Fenster and Rueben had the snake boots on. It hadn't escaped his attention that he and Griff hadn't been provided any. For that matter, neither had Brick or Ike. But then, he wouldn't have been terribly surprised if Brick just bit a rattlesnake or killed it in a flash with one of his knives.

They started off along the road, having to do their usual dash off into the brush every time a pair of headlights started coming their direction from either side. Traffic wasn't heavy though enough was there to keep them surging off and back on to the road often, a right pain. That was on top of Budge wondering if he would end up standing on a snake. Once, a lizard took off as Brick shoved him into a stand of sumac, and his heart was beating like a jackhammer for the next few minutes.

FENSTER TURNED THE white truck into a nearly obscured lane at the edge of a property.

"How do you know the owner won't decide to come back down this lane instead of his main one? He could bump into us," Griff said from the back seat.

"Because I scouted this place as well as the other one Brick's team is using. This one hasn't been used in years and leads down to an abandoned boat ramp on the shore with more than half its concrete washed away, so it's unusable."

When Fenster stopped the truck, Griff got out of the back seat and went to the truck bed to pick up a grill. He already knew what they needed to do. It was as if they had done a dress rehearsal before, when Fenster managed to get bitten by a rattlesnake.

Griff did keep his eyes open and kept the fine cone tip of his penlight beam scouting the woods floor as he carried the grill to where Rueben could set them up in the row they wanted, just out of the range of the detectors but where the wiggle of flames would show later.

Rueben came limping along with the box of flares. If it came to a footrace out of there, Griff figured he could get at least a few steps on Rueben.

As he went back to the truck to get another grill, he saw Fenster waiting on him. He must have read Griff's mind about finding a chance to take off running.

Griff swallowed hard and picked up two grills and started back toward the woods.

AL CAME IN THE FRONT door with plastic bags of groceries in each arm.

"Oh, bless you," Bonnie said. "We weren't starving and having to resort to cannibalism yet, but it was getting nip and tuck." She was on the living room floor, bent over beside Little Al, who was playing with a toy that had a steering wheel and simulated the dashboard of a car, even to a gear shift and turn signal. From the way he was wildly wrenching the wheel around, he would have knocked every other vehicle in the state off the road and probably picked off one or two steers that wandered too close.

"You shouldn't think that," Maury said. "Cannibals usually go for the well-rounded one first."

"Give Al a hand bringing in the groceries from his truck," Fergie said, "before you get yourself in a hole too deep to dig out from."

Once Maury hustled out the front door, Fergie asked, "Did you have any luck finding what could help Clayton?"

"I did indeed, and you can bet the old boy will be positively turning cartwheels around the department parking lot when he hears what I found out. I've been calling him and calling him, but he's out of pocket for the moment, and no one seems to know where he is. The one time I would really like to talk with him, and he's as gone as Houdini."

Bonnie picked up Little Al and held him close as she went over to start taking groceries out of the bags. "Oh, good. You really stocked up on breakfast stuff. Tell you what—late as it is, I'm gonna whip you up the best breakfast you've had in a spell. But what's this?" She held up a package and waved it in the air. "For the life of me, I don't understand the idea of turkey bacon."

"It's to help keep us thin," Fergie said.

"You can see it's not working on me." Bonnie patted her round belly. "Now, when you find me a turkey that's producing pork belly, then I'll subscribe."

"Here. I'll do it." Fergie had been trying to convert Bonnie to healthier foods for some time and had been making little headway because, left to Bonnie, they would've been having biscuits and gravy every morning. "All turkey bacon needs is to be microwaved between a couple of paper towels." Fergie reached for the package.

"Might as well cook the cardboard with it so it'll all taste the same." Bonnie gave a huff and a toss of her head that sent her blond curls bouncing around. "With your way, we sure miss out on the sizzle of fat in the pan."

"It's the fat in the pan I'm worried about," Fergie said.

"It's nice to know we're one cozy family all together and enjoying life again," Maury said as he came in the door, carrying the rest of the groceries.

Tanner rose from the floor to follow him across the room, acting hopeful that something in those bags might be for him.

BUDGE GAVE A SIGH WHEN at last they got away from the road after many moments of dodging off and back on again. They made their way to the spot they'd been before, out of range of the motion-detecting cameras. Ike had been carrying his pistol in his left hand, perhaps not trusting his right yet. He shoved the .357 inside his belt as he headed off with his roll of duct tape to come in around behind the first camera. Maybe Budge had broken a bone or two in Ike's hand. If so, he didn't feel bad at all about doing it. Brick stayed a wary distance from him, far enough away that his hand could dart inside his jacket if needed.

They waited and watched until they could just barely see Ike reach around the trunk of the tree and cover the lens with tape. He eased back into the woods and headed down to where the next camera hung on a tree.

Brick and Budge stood where they were until Brick judged enough time had gone by to have at least the three nearest cameras disabled. Then Brick gave him a nudge.

"C'mon, you lump. Let's get started. Move along quickly, and cover all the ground you need to as fast as you can."

Budge slipped the headphones on and turned on the detector. The first rule of using a detector, he'd learned, was to always have it on and be sweeping, no matter where you were headed, because you just never knew.

He moved the search coil back and forth across the ground, ignoring any little pings, waiting to come across a monstrously huge target, one that would just about blast his eardrums out. That would be the gold.

Budge was moving faster and not because Brick was staying close and prodding him along. He had some of the original thrill of the hunt going on and expected at any moment to come across the buried treasure they sought, at the same time knowing that its discovery would probably mark the end of him. Hitting a target of that size would send out an alarm past the headphones that even Brick would hear.

He followed the map in his head of what he had covered and what the old dude he'd seen had covered. With a certain sadness, he knew when he was done, that he'd covered it all. But he kept going, milking the moment, trying to stretch out the last few moments of his life.

Brick reached out and grabbed Budge's shoulder. He leaned close and looked hard into Budge's eyes.

Budge shook his head and turned off the detector, pulled the headphones off, and hung them from the machine right beside the trowel. He wanted to be able to drop the whole thing if he had to take off and run as fast as he could, knowing he would probably only get a few steps.

"We've got one more place to check."

Budge shrugged.

"The house. We need to check there. Maybe they already found the damned stuff." Brick reached for his phone. He called Fenster first. "You'd better get started with things on your end."

He hung up and glanced at Budge, probably deciding something trivial in his mind, like whether Budge got to live a few more minutes. Brick lifted his phone and called Ike. "C'mon back. It's time for the house."

When he hung up, he stood staring at Budge, deciding something.

This is it, Budge thought. *Tick. Tick. Tick.* Whatever happens will probably happen fast.

"Do you think if you wave that thing around inside the house, that might be able to find where any gold is hid?" Brick asked.

"I can try," Budge said.

"Okay. We'll give that a shot."

Budge let out a long, slow breath.

Chapter Twenty-Eight

"Take it easy. Go very slow, or there's the slightest chance you'll set off one of those motion detectors," Fenster said. He was staying back, watching as they moved each grill up into place.

With each passing moment, Griff was more aware that he could be in the final moments of his life. He started moving in exaggerated slow motion, probably looking like time-lapse photography.

"Hey, knock that off, wiseacre. Just be careful. Get them up to that line I marked the last time, and then we wait."

Griff dropped the one he held into place and turned to go back to the truck for another.

He had figured out how their end of the ploy was supposed to work. If Brick needed attention taken away from the other side of the property, he'd let them know, and they'd light flares and pop them into the grills. From a distance and through the faraway lenses of the motion detectors, it could look like the woods were on fire. There was no danger of a real brush fire that could threaten them and maybe keep them from getting clear. But they'd have a jump on whoever came to fight the fire. They would just have to get in the truck and cut the hell out of there while Brick did whatever he had in mind on the other side.

What scalded Griff's preserves was that even if they got all the gold, he and Budge would get nothing unless they counted a bullet each.

When everything was in place, they went back to the truck, leaned on its side, and waited. One of them was on either side of Griff. The night felt unusually quiet although Griff could hear the occasional scuffle of dried leaves on the woods floor—a lizard, he hoped. The wind made one dried limb scratch against another in a creaking grind. He figured if the woods ever did catch fire, dry as it was, the flames would sweep across and reduce everything low to ashes in very little time. Also, a little breeze would fan the flames of any blaze. He'd seen grass fires before that looked possessed, they moved so quickly. He licked one finger and held it up, trying to figure if any wildfire would want to come their way.

"What the hell are you doing?"

He put his hand back down and wiped his finger across his jeans.

Wait. Wait. Wait. Just sit and wait.

Then Fenster's phone rang. "Okay." He hung up and turned to them. "It's time to rock and roll."

"FUNNY WE HAVEN'T SEEN any wildlife movement at all for a spell." Maury waved a hand at the left side of the TV screen that took the feed from the cameras. "Usually, we see a coyote or possum by now."

"That does seem a little odd." Al got up from the dining table and came over to look closer.

Bonnie glanced up from where she was on the floor with Little Al.

Fergie said, "Maybe we ought to go take a—"

Before she could say "look," flickers of flame began to dance behind the trunks of trees.

"Fire!" Maury yelled. "There's a fire out there."

In a burst Al, Fergie, and Maury headed for the door. Fergie and Al each grabbed a pistol, while Maury snatched up the Winchester Model 12 that leaned by the front door.

"Hey, what about me?" Bonnie shouted. "I'm the best shot of all of us."

"You and Tanner watch the house and Little Al," Maury said. "I suspect this is more than just a wildfire."

Al made sure they each had a couple of pairs of handcuffs in their back pockets.

They took off running once they were out the front door.

Al had his phone out, automatically calling the sheriff's department first. "Gonna need some fire trucks out at my place," he said once he identified himself. "Clayton doesn't happen to be there, does he? I didn't think so."

Maury realized that none of them had paused to grab flashlights. As they ran through the woods, thorny bushes grabbed at their clothes and arms. They had no time to pause and be more careful.

As he got closer, he thought he saw the shapes of figures moving behind the flames, and he wondered for a second if the local volunteer fire department was already on the scene, battling the blaze. Then he realized the forms were moving rapidly away, getting smaller until he could no longer see them.

Fergie's long legs had her in the lead by the time they got to the flames. Al and Maury weren't far behind. For a second, Maury slowed as he realized what he was seeing. A row of small red grills stood in a line just outside the edge of the property. The first word that sprang to mind was "Trap!"

He raised the shotgun he held and jacked a shell into the chamber, carrying it in both hands as he moved forward.

Al and Fergie had their pistols up and pointed ahead.

They wove their way past the flares which were sending up light and smoke from the grills and kept running.

For the glitter of a second, Maury had one thought: "Bonnie." But he kept running, feeling his legs and lungs struggling as he tried to keep up with Fergie and Al.

Chapter Twenty-Nine

Nelson Jeremiah parked his year-old dark-blue Silverado in a far corner of the parking lot, almost out of range of the mercury vapor lights casting a ghastly blue glow over the asphalt with the black night squeezing but not getting in. He got out and took a two-gallon can of gas from the back. He started across the lot, trying to look not furtive but as natural as possible, keeping the can low and pressed against his leg. Before leaving his house, he'd considered wearing ninja black for only half a second and had dismissed that. He would be far more invisible wearing the royal-blue jacket he wore most days as a sheriff's department captain.

Running a casual hand across his closely cropped gray hair, he strolled with a relaxed gait across one lot then another as he approached the small data building where files were kept.

Even though he had been in heated shoot-outs and gravel-skidding car chases, he couldn't recall when his heart had been beating with such animation.

Slow and steady does it. In a minute, I'll be done and out of here.

He'd turned off the security camera to the area. He had the rank and clearance to accomplish that without any kind of fuss.

The sheriff's department at night was never quite a ghost town. Vehicles were always coming and going. An occasional siren sounded in the distance. The maintenance building was not active, but dispatchers were, sitting by their mics and ready for the usual flurry of DWIs, domestic quarrels, or anything else that might need attention in a county as big as Travis.

His footsteps ticked across the empty lot quietly, neither making a great deal of clatter nor being furtively silent—he was just someone going about his business. He glanced left and right while steadily moving toward the small information building where data was kept.

He stopped at the door, took the key out with his right hand, and turned it in the lock with a small metallic rasp. With the door open, he unscrewed the lid to the can, took out a book of matches from his pocket, and started to step through, then half a dozen harsh spotlights snapped on, and four deputies in SWAT uniforms came around to point the barrels of Bushmaster .223 rifles directly at him.

Sheriff Clayton himself stepped around the corner of the building. He was dressed in full uniform. "Time to step down, Nelson. You know I'm getting too old for stakeouts, so let's move this along."

"You've got nothing. Maybe entrapment or, at the most, a witch hunt."

"The thing about witch hunts is that occasionally there's a witch. You're done here."

"You've got nothing on me."

"Attempted arson for a starter."

"This?" Nelson held up the can. "It's for my lawn mower."

"Unless there's a lawn mower inside that building, your story doesn't hold water."

"You've got nothing," Nelson said, with less conviction.

"I knew you'd hear somehow that Al Quinn and Meat Jenkins were messing about this building where someone—you, we think—erased some records. On the chance you didn't get them all, I've needed to be staked out here myself. We have film of you buying the gas and coming right here. Every step you took is recorded. Take him away."

Nelson shoved his right hand inside his jacket and barely got his fist around the butt of his gun before two members of the SWAT team had his hand twisted behind his back and were shoving him face down to the ground.

"I told you he might try to eat his gun," Clayton said.

"Right you were," said Eddie Wilton, the SWAT team captain. "By the way, I heard your old friend Al Quinn has been trying to get in touch with you."

Clayton took out his phone and hit the number then shook his head. "Hmm. Now *he* won't answer."

As they were taking Nelson away, he yelled back over his shoulder, "This isn't over!"

Clayton shook his head. "Truer words have never been spoke."

Chapter Thirty

The flares were the kind Griff could twist the cap off and rub its end briskly across the coarse striking surface of the cap. He lit three, getting each into a grill. Rueben and Fenster got all the others going until a wall of flames shot up that should look like a forest fire when seen through the lenses of the motion-detector cameras.

As soon as they had them all lit, they took off in a run, heading back toward the truck.

He glanced back in time to see the hobbling Rueben stumble. The Uzi strap over his shoulder had tangled with his legs as he fell, knocking over one of the grills holding a flare.

Fenster rushed over to him to help him to his feet. Little flames began to crackle up in the loose leaf litter and twigs on the forest floor. Fenster tried to stamp at them while holding Rueben upright. But the flames were spreading.

This is your chance, Griff told himself. He broke into as hard a run as he ever had in his life.

"Hey!" Fenster shouted. "Stop!"

That only goaded Griff to run even faster.

He got to the truck, opened the driver's side door, and got in.

The other two had to ignore the growing fire and rush to the truck, pursuing Griff. Rueben was limping worse than ever as Fenster tugged him along toward the truck.

As they got to it, Griff locked the doors from inside.

Fenster grabbed at the handle, couldn't open the door, and looked through the glass at Griff. "What the hell? Open the blasted door."

Griff just stared back at him.

"Open the damned door, I say!" Fenster pounded at the window for a moment then got out his key and put it in the door.

Every time he twisted the key and got the door unlocked, Griff locked it again. *Open. Shut. Open. Shut.*

Griff could see people come running out of the woods in their direction.

"Aw, shoot out the window!" Fenster yelled at Rueben.

Rueben started to lift the Uzi, but the ones running toward them were almost there and they were shooting.

Rueben spun around to aim at them instead.

THE FIRST SMALL CRACKLING wave of fire was just beginning to spread from the fallen grill as Al, Fergie, and Maury ran out through the tail end of the woods past the other flare-lit grills. As much as they wanted to pause and put out the fire, they ran on after those escaping.

As they got within sight of the ones they were after, the three of them knew to spread out as they ran toward the truck.

One of the men they faced was lifting an Uzi, squeezing the trigger as he did, wildly firing shots into the ground then at them.

Both Al and Fergie dove to the ground, rolled, and came up with the pistols ready to shoot. But Maury, who was less experienced, stayed upright and shot while on the run.

Bullets tossed up puffs of dirt as the Uzi spat out a rattle of shots right at them.

The guy with the Uzi probably had his eye drawn to the brisk drop and roll Al and Fergie had performed. He might have discounted poor Maury, who had stopped and stood there while firing his shotgun. He probably didn't look too formidable. But overlooking poor Maury was always a mistake.

His advantage was he had a pump shotgun he knew how to use. He fired three times at the man with the Uzi, who dropped his gun and crumpled to the ground. He'd been hit in the left leg by one of Maury's shots.

"Damn. I've been halfway kilt again." He rolled on the ground, holding his leg while screaming in pain.

The man standing outside the truck raised his hands high, showing no gun.

The one inside the truck raised his hands as well.

As they came up to the truck, the wounded guy on the ground yelled, "Kill them, you chickenshits!"

The man by the truck held out his wrists, and Fergie tugged a pair of cuffs out of her back pocket and clamped them on, turning him around so his hands were behind him. He complied with her every directive nudge.

Al yanked the Uzi away from the reach of the guy on the ground, tossing it aside. He and Maury flipped him over, ignoring screams and curses that would have embarrassed any dozen sailors.

The guy inside the truck opened the door and came outside with his hands high. "My name's Griff. I'm glad you saved me. They were going to kill me as soon as they found what they were looking for."

Al turned him around. As he was slapping on a pair of cuffs as quickly as he could, he asked, "And what the hell was that? What were you guys all looking for?"

The sound of sirens approaching came from the distance.

"They both work for Moog Palance."

"We know who he is," Fergie said. "A low-level loan shark."

"We owed him money, were going to pay him back when we found it."

"Found what?" Impatient, Al was close to shouting. "Why are you here? What are you trying to find on my property?"

"The gold."

"What gold?"

"Buried gold from back when this was a stagecoach station. We had a letter that said this was where it is."

"Well, I don't know where it is now, but it's not on my property. At my request, my friend Huff went over the place from stem to stern with the very best detector available, one he'd built himself, and said there's not a thing worth finding anywhere."

Griff's head hung for a moment. When he looked up, he said, "Then we were wrong and have been about a number of things."

Al and Fergie took out more cuffs and handcuffed the three of them to each other, letting the wounded one anchor them. He still struggled while the other two sat on the ground beside him, their faces resigned.

"You won't be so calm if the fire spreads this way," Fergie said.

"Get their pants," Al said.

Fergie and Maury looked at him, eyes opening wider.

"To fight the fire."

They tugged off the men's boots and shoes then yanked the pants off all three, getting screams from the downed one when they exposed his wound and scraped it in the process.

"Where are the rest of you?" Al snapped as he stood, holding the pair of bloody jeans.

"They said something about going into the house," Griff said.

Al glanced toward Maury, who spun and took off at a run, holding his shotgun. His wife and child were back there, alone.

"You got these guys?" Al asked Fergie.

"If they twitch, I'll start by shooting this one in the head." She kept her pistol pointed at Rueben, who quit squirming and froze in place, blood still oozing from his leg.

"I'll send an ambulance and any deputies I can over this way as soon as I can. If the volunteer firefighters arrive first, you know where to send them." Al spun and took off at a run back toward the growing fire, fighting down an ugly, scared feeling in the pit of his stomach and hoping Bonnie and Little Al were alive.

At the edge of the growing ring of fire, he held the leg ends of two pants and slapped at the flames as fast as he could, careful not to throw up sparks or fan the flames. At least the breeze wasn't strong. Otherwise, the fire would be rolling like a wave.

Al was torn and tugged in three directions, the house, Fergie, and the fire. The moral dilemma was real. He knew, though, that if he didn't stay and do what he could to stop the fire, it could sweep all the way to engulf the house and possibly kill the ones there anyway, and that would most certainly do the house a bit of no good. Bonnie and Maury were both armed but were up against three tough hombres. Still, he had to count on them and stay to do what he could about a spreading fire.

He heard a siren getting louder and closer and hoped that was the volunteer fire department.

That faint hope made a huge leap when he saw Randy Ray Boyd running his way in full firefighting gear with half a dozen others behind him. He was in his late seventies but still loved the thrill of fighting fires though he'd come within an ace of losing his own life in a grass fire while Al was still on the sheriff's department. The big plus was that he lived just eight miles down the road from Al.

"Man, I am glad to see you!" Al shouted.

Randy came right around to the downwind side of the fire, where Al was swatting away with the tattered and smoldering jeans. "You caught this just in time and before the wind picked up." He sprayed a fire retardant, working quickly along the line where the fire was advancing. A couple of the firemen were dragging the end of a hose and would soon have it charged and throwing water.

"You guys going to be able to handle this? I've got to run to the house and help there."

"Sure. Do what you gotta do, Al." Boyd kept spraying but gave Al what was probably meant to be a broad wink. "You oughta know, though, that Fergie back there's already got the pants off those men. My guys just about fell down laughing when we got here, as did the first deputy to arrive."

Al shook his head and spun to take off running toward the house.

Chapter Thirty-One

The house seemed empty as they got closer, its lights dim against the black of night. Budge hoped it was. Brick held his pistol and looked eager to use it. Budge had no weapon. He carried the metal detector in one hand and doubted very much it would be any use as a club, and it was expensive enough he didn't want to break it, though he might if that was what it took to get away.

A wind swept across them, rattling a few dead limbs high in a nearby tree as well. To Budge's stretched nerves, they sounded like dry bones clacking together. He almost held a finger up to his lips for the wind to be still. His nerves were strung that tight at the moment, and he wasn't quite making sense to himself. They were trying to be so quiet, looking around all the while.

Budge didn't like this idea at all, breaking into someone's home.

They eased around the lit windows of the upper floor, the drapes drawn, and went down the hill together to the downstairs back porch to stand in front of that door. He stayed close behind Ike, who eased up and felt the doorknob.

Ike had to put the Ruger he'd been holding in his left hand inside his belt to take out a wire to pick the lock. It took him a while because he had to use his bad right hand, but at last, he had it ready to open.

Brick held his pistol ready. He nodded. Ike tumbled the lock open and twisted the knob, opening the door.

A woman at the far end of the room had her back turned to them. She was holding a small boy in her arms, and his arms were waving and feet kicking in a full-out squirm. He must have seen the pistol Brick was pointing in their direction as they entered the room and started that way.

"Pow. Pow," the boy said. "Bang."

BONNIE SPUN AND SAW them. She wore her fuzzy pink robe and could feel the weight of her peashooter, the Chiefs Special she carried in the front pocket as often as she felt it was needed. She had just picked up Little Al to put him in his crib when the three men burst in through the back door. They had only recently switched Little Al over to a baby crib tent that zipped closed on top of his crib since he'd been getting out and roaming at night. After a couple of times waking to find him staring at them in bed, they'd made the change.

"Where's the gold?" asked the black-bearded, mean-as-a-snake-looking man pointing the gun.

"What the hell're you talking about?"

"You haven't found it? Well, maybe we will. Budge here is going to give the place a quick sweep with a metal detector." He nodded toward the big one of them.

"Knock yourself out." Bonnie recognized the gadget Maury had been so keen about. But this puzzle had way too many pieces to make any kind of sense to her.

She heard Tanner coming slowly down the stairs, growling with his teeth bared. He might have been old, but he still had a heart as big as the house and more than enough courage.

"Brick!" the other big guy with his pistol inside his belt yelled.

Brick started to swing his gun toward Tanner.

"Don't you dare hurt that dog!" The biggest guy dropped the metal detector to the floor and reached for Brick with lightning-quick hands.

Bonnie could hear the fingers of that hand crackling and popping as the bones shattered like so much popcorn.

She swung Little Al over his crib and let him drop, then she went for the pistol in her pocket.

As she tugged it out, the other gun clattered to the floor after falling from Brick's mangled hand. Budge had him by the wrist and was twisting, but Brick managed to get his left hand inside his jacket. He yanked out a knife and stabbed it into Budge's shoulder.

The big guy hardly flinched. He kept twisting, bending Brick to the red-carpeted floor.

Bonnie stepped forward and put the barrel of her little snub-nosed gun almost to Brick's knee and pulled the trigger.

He screamed and fell to the floor.

The other guy was struggling to get a bulky Ruger out from under his belt and had just got it free to lift and aim it when she shot him in the left shoulder and fired again at his thigh. Something in the pant leg of his jeans made a metal clang when the bullet went through. A wrench and a slim jim tumbled out of a hole in his jeans and clattered to the floor.

He rocked back and dropped his gun. "What the hell?" His hands reached up to try to press against his leg and shoulder wounds at the same time.

"The next one's in the crotch. Drop and sit on the floor."

He did so with eyes open wide and began to moan as his hands pressed tighter. He swayed in place and moaned.

Bonnie kicked the fallen Ruger out of reach over into a corner then did the same with Brick's Colt .45, which lay on the floor.

She turned to Budge. "You're not gonna give me any trouble, are you?"

"I'm on your side, lady. You just saved my life. Just a minute, though."

Brick was trying to get his left hand inside his jacket again. She had seen eyes like that on a hurt feral cat that had biting and clawing in mind instead of letting anyone help it.

Budge pounded the top of his head with a hammer of a fist, and Brick crumpled to the floor into the growing pool of his own blood.

Gonna have a dickens of a time getting blood out of this red carpet, she thought. She knew it would turn brown and stain if she didn't get right to cleaning it up soon.

"This other guy is Ike, and I'd keep a careful eye on him."

"We can always let Tanner have a go at him too," Bonnie said.

Tanner had a grip on Brick's pant leg and was growling and shaking his head.

Ike's wide eyes moved from her, to the dog, to Brick, and to Budge, who was lowering the metal detector to the floor. Ike kept moaning and bleeding.

Budge slowly pulled the knife from his shoulder and tossed it to one side. Blood seeped from the wound.

"Doesn't that hurt?"

"Only when I laugh." He grinned at her. "I'm just light-headed to be alive. That guy there"—he nodded toward Brick—"was going to kill me if Ike here didn't beat him to it."

Little Al was awake and calling out to her. But he would have to wait. She went over to make sure he stayed in his crib, but she kept her hand down by her side with her gun in it.

"I'm a nurse. Let me get my things, and I'll do what I can to patch you up."

"What about those guys?"

"Screw them. Their attitudes about life were all wrong."

Ike moaned louder.

Bonnie kept her black bag in the small wooden stand by the head of the bed. She got it out with one hand and came over to Budge. "Tear your shirt open."

He did as she asked.

Her nursing and nurturing nature said this big lug in front of her needed help first. She tore open a gauze pad and pressed it against his wound.

"Here, hold that in place." Bonnie reached into the bag for a role of zinc oxide tape. "Now, what's the cockamamie about gold?" Bonnie asked.

"It's kind of a long story," Budge said. "And I'm not sure we'll have time for it."

Footsteps came pounding down the steps, and Maury burst into the room. His face was flushed an unusually bright red, and he was breathing hard. He pointed the shotgun he held at Budge, the only male left standing.

"Don't shoot him," Bonnie said. "He might just turn out to be one of the good guys. You can shoot these other two if the bloodlust is still upon you, but they already have holes in them."

When the barrel of Maury's shotgun swung toward him, Ike moaned even louder and stared at the end of the barrel. Brick was still as out of it as plaid disco pants from the sixties and lay unconscious on the carpet with blood seeping from his knee.

Bonnie slipped her Chiefs Special back into the pocket of her robe and finished dressing Budge's wound.

Chapter Thirty-Two

Victor Kahlon wove his way through the early-morning Austin streets, following the directions from his GPS, which had a voice he found bossy at times. The chain-link gate was open, the unlocked padlock swinging from the latch. He pulled into the parking lot and saw Lt. Harley Jenson's unmarked car, a white Crown Vic of course because Harley was pretty old school. He stood outside the vehicle with two uniformed city cops.

Victor got out and nodded toward the battleship-gray Lincoln Town Car parked by the warehouse door.

"Who belongs to that?"

"The tags come back to Moog Palance, a fellow with whom we are quite familiar, a bottom-feeding shyster who does a bit of loan sharking." Harley was tall and ramrod slim and kept his gray hair cut into a short flattop although it was threatening to march back farther onto his dome of a head. "Who'd you get the tip on this place from?"

"A couple of guys who felt they needed to do some trading up to cut a deal."

"Hmm. Now what?"

"We wait."

Victor moved closer so he could lean on the side of the Crown Vic.

They didn't have to wait long. Ten minutes later, the warehouse door opened, and a man came out wearing a suit and carrying a pigskin briefcase in one hand and a set of keys in the other. He turned to lock the door and froze when he saw the two uniformed cops rushing toward him, both with sidearms drawn and pointed at him. Still, he made a play for it, dropping the briefcase and keys while reaching inside his suit jacket.

The three of them wrestled upright for a moment, one of the cops coming out with the guy's gun while the other got an arm twisted behind the man's back. They had the cuffs on him when they brought him over to Harley's car.

"Empty his pockets."

The cops put the objects on the hood of the car. Aside from a wallet, another set of keys, and some bills, they found a black cord with two wooden handles.

They opened the orange pigskin briefcase. It was filled with bundles of hundred-dollar bills.

"Hmmm," Harley said.

Victor nodded.

"I own building. Lawyer." They were the first words the man had spoken, and he seemed to be having an issue relearning English. "I want lawyer. Now!"

"This is a jasper named Semion Kashov. He does, in fact, own the building, but he's not ours to play with."

"Diplomatic immunity," Kashov managed, glaring at them.

"He is *not* a diplomat," Harley said. "More like the opposite. But we don't have to worry about that."

As if on cue, three black SUVs rolled in so close together that their bumpers were nearly touching. They stopped in a row, and men poured out, all dressed to play in their black FBI flak jackets and other SWAT gear.

"It's open!" Harley yelled at them, rather spoiling the fun of the two at the front with the steel battering ram.

They swung the door open wide and poured in.

Harley smiled at Victor.

In a few minutes, one of them came back to the door and yelled over to Harley, "There's a dead guy in here."

Harley shrugged and started that way. "I'll take a look."

He came back out barely a minute or two later, on the phone and talking to his ME. Harley put the phone away and leaned back beside Victor. "It's Moog. Garroted."

"Doesn't look too good for Kashov, does it?"

"Clarkson, who's the special agent running this gung ho bunch, says Kashov had a reservation on a flight to Rio. They're as tickled as punch about this whole thing and, I suspect, will take credit for busting a pretty large trucking-theft outfit."

"Power to them," Victor said. "Would have been just so much more paperwork for us."

After a while, an agent came out with a handful of men crowded behind him. He strutted toward them.

"That's Clarkson," Harley said in a low voice.

Clarkson waved a hand to the men with him, and they swooped in and took Kashov, his wallet as well as his gun, and the briefcase, leaving the garrote for Harley's ME.

"Good to work with you again, Lieutenant." Clarkson held out a hand to shake. "We'll seal this off and take possession. You're welcome to the body you said is a local citizen."

"Not one of your upstanding Kiwanis club sorts," Harley said, "but he did live in Austin."

Clarkson gave a quick glance, sweeping over Victor and the two uniformed cops, spun on his heel, and headed for the line of black SUVs.

"Ever regret not going federal, Harley?" Victor asked.

"Not so much as you might think." Harley grinned.

Chapter Thirty-Three

Clayton went over to the county jail building, the biggest in the sheriff's department complex, and the turnkey had the one called Budge waiting in a single room with one wrist handcuffed to the steel table bolted to the cement floor. Clayton slid onto the steel bench across from the guy, who sure filled out his striped pants and shirt.

"Thanks for not cutting my hair. It's not much, but I take pride in it."

Clayton pursed his lips for a moment, mostly to keep from laughing. He'd grown up around many a redneck sporting a mullet, and Budge sure enough had him a classic mullet head.

Outside the room, the clang of bars closing and the low murmur of voices with an occasional shout went on as usual. As a rookie deputy, Clayton had spent a year working the jail, which was the norm then. That was so long in the past that he could hardly remember, yet the sounds were forever familiar.

"How do you like it here so far?"

"Well, the food's better than I thought it'd be. But then, I was pretty hungry when I got here. Griff hates the outfits, though. He's a bit of a dandy, if you want to know the truth."

"Do you like the idea of getting to spend many more years in an institution like this?"

"No. Definitely nope."

"Well, that's where you're likely headed unless you're willing to put the skids on your ways and turn your life around. Are you willing?"

"Yep. Sure am... sir."

"Why do they call you Budge when your real name is Malcolm Malloy?"

"I think you can see the obvious, and my folks were in a right mood when they named me Malcolm, drunk maybe."

"You were mixed up in some pretty serious stuff here."

"And darned lucky to come out alive. Those guys had every intention of killing Griff and I when they got what they wanted." He reached up with his free hand to sweep his hair up higher off his forehead.

"They were indeed some nasty ones, especially that Brick. Bonnie was lucky you were handy when you were. Usually, she can take care of herself and would have turned him into Swiss cheese with her pistol if they hadn't caught her with her child in her arms."

"She patched me up real nice before the ambulance guys got to me. I owe her plenty. I'm glad her kid's okay... and the dog. I like dogs."

"Well, you did them all a favor."

"I was glad for the chance even though I didn't think about it much in the moment, just did what I had to."

"Let's loop back to the beginning. You and your pal Griff were on some shaky ground, sneaking onto Al Quinn's property to poke around at night without asking."

Budge lowered his head. When he looked up he said, "I guess greed got the best of us there. We had a letter that said gold was buried on the place when it was a stagecoach station. If we told the owner, we couldn't rightly keep it. So Griff thought it best if we just got the gold and skedaddled. It made a certain kind of sense at the time... to us. I know now we were wrong, especially after the way that Brick fellow went about it."

"Well, I've seen the letter. I can see why you two were het up about the notion. But you know you could have gone to the property owner, Al Quinn, and suggested some kind of split."

"That seems a wiser idea now." Budge glanced around at the walls and down at his jail garb. "I guess I was swayed by Griff at first. He made it sound like the folks would just say no and find the gold themselves."

"I want you to realize that if I pushed, I could hold you both on trespassing charges. But Al is willing to let that slide since you both helped him and his when the moment was right, and I kind of owe Al a favor at the moment, a big one. But it would all depend on whether you are both contrite and have learned something here."

"Sir, I can't tell you when I've learned more, and I'm something of a pretty steady reader. But I'd rather be publicly spanked in the nude before I'd go through that again. I've never feared for my life as much... ever."

"It sounds like you have some regrets."

"I do."

"Are you remorseful about anything else?"

"Well, once... I probably shouldn't talk about this. Might get me in trouble. Griff said never to mention it."

"Try me."

"Well, this once, a guy in the far-back darkish corner of the parking lot of The Twisted Rope two-stepping kicker bar tried to mug Griff, and I stopped him but was kind of rough doing it."

"That solves a riddle from a while back for me. The so-called victim was a character known as E. Z. Thatcher, who we estimate had mugged over twenty people in that and other parking lots at night. At the time, did you feel you were acting in self-defense?"

"Well, he meant to hurt Griff. I guess I acted on his behalf, maybe got a little too rough. Like I said, Griff said we shouldn't ever talk about it."

"I'm glad you did. What I'm after here is the notion of whether you are willing to turn over a new leaf and work for a living if you get the chance. Are you?"

Budge tilted his head and seemed to give the idea some serious thought. "You know, I'd be okay with that if I could just get a good start. It always seemed we were behind, could never catch up."

"I have an idea about that if you're willing to go along."

"I would. Believe me, I just want a fair chance."

"First of all, I want you to know that Moog is dead. So you guys have a clean slate there."

"Whew. Really?"

"The other thing is that this Brick fellow that you subdued and helped us capture had a price on his head, a reward. It's for ten thousand dollars, and I could put you both in for it. But it would take a while to process."

"Do you mean we found a treasure after all?"

"Sort of. Now if you're genuinely willing to go straight—"

"I am."

"I'm willing to help you both get jobs where your employers would understand your pasts, and you'd have to stay out of trouble or deal with me."

"Got you."

"I'm willing to advance you each a thousand dollars, out of my pocket, against the reward money you'll get. You have to pay it back—it's just a get-by loan—but there'll be no vig. I'm no Moog. Understand?"

Budge nodded.

Clayton stood up and started for the door. After he took only a couple of steps, Budge spoke.

"Sir, there's something I want you to do with that thousand you have earmarked for me."

Clayton turned around slowly. "And what's that?"

"There's this little old lady that lives out alone by herself. I don't know her name or address, but she had a dog named Chico. I want you to give her three hundred dollars out of my thousand if you can find her."

Clayton grinned broadly in spite of himself. "Her name is Francis Sullivan, and she filed a burglary report. You guys didn't leave a single fingerprint. The first thing she thought about was that her little dog was okay."

"He was one brave little fellow."

"Let me ask, in the way of a job, is there anything you're good at or like to be around, besides dogs?"

"Well, I like to read."

CLAYTON GAVE THEM TIME to talk between themselves. When he came in the door later for his session with Griff Fielding, he found him rubbing at a green spot on his wrist and looking disdainfully at his jail garb.

He looked up at the sheriff. His face still showed a hint of the bruises from where he'd taken a beating. He would have a scar for life where his arm had been cut by Brick's knife.

"If it makes you feel better, Brick had a green spot just like that on his wrist that he won't see fade soon, and he'll probably go through the rest of his life with a permanent limp, thanks to Bonnie. He's a scrappy one, by the way, and was quite a handful until those New Mexico folks took him away. He's their headache now. I suspect there's a little bias over that way, and they may come down quite hard on him."

"Good. He was an awful, awful man."

"I take it you don't want to be associated with that sort again."

"No. Never."

"And?"

"Budge told me about the deal. It sounds great. All we want is a start, to get by while we ease into that sort of life. I already heard from my squeeze, Tyrza Floen, that she's headed off for a new life herself with some boot salesman from El Paso. I guess life's about change. Budge told me you'd be on us like stink if we didn't toe the line."

"He's right about that. Now, this is a bit like AA, where you fess up to things you regret. Are you ready for that?"

"I think you'd better bring me a pad and something to write with. I've got a few things itching at my conscience, up to and including my Uncle Leo."

"I'll bet this is going to be good." Clayton stood and started for the door.

"Oh, and there's one other thing."

Clayton turned around. "What's that?"

"There's this little old lady. I can tell you how to get to her house."

"Budge didn't tell you about Francis Sullivan. That's the lady's name."

"No. But I want you to help me do right by her. Could you see that she gets four hundred dollars of the thousand you were going to give me? My conscience would feel ever so much better."

"Are you certain that's the amount you took from her?"

"I know it's not. It's more than we took. But mark some of that down to repentance."

Clayton suppressed a grin. "Okay, then. I'll be back with paper and a pen."

As he went out the door and closed it behind himself, Clayton muttered to himself, "Well, hope springs eternal. I expected him to be the harder nut to crack here."

Chapter Thirty-Four

Al swung the door open, and there stood Sheriff Clayton. He was wearing a smile as bright and shiny as a new penny and just as welcome to Al. Clayton's suit coat was the same brown as the uniform he wore at work, the white shirt open at the collar. The rest was jeans over boots and the usual white cowboy hat. Al wondered for a split second if the outfit was a conscious effort to look different from what Nelson had been wearing for the recent while. Clayton usually wore a blue sport coat himself.

"Sorry I didn't get out to visit sooner, but it's been a busy week. Does Bonnie have any of her excellent coffee in a pot?"

"And some fresh-made biscuits and a pan of gravy!" Bonnie yelled from the kitchen, where she hovered over the stove.

Tanner got up and came over to give Clayton's pant leg a friendly nip.

"I hear you've been up to your usual home defense." Clayton bent to pat Tanner on the head.

Tanner looked up, sharing what could pass for a smile while wagging his tail.

Still bent forward, Clayton looked up at Al. "I'm glad your lot only clipped a few feathers this time. Put all but one of them in the hospital, mind you. But they're alive. Most of them are singing like a choir, too, except that one they call Brick. No need for him to talk. There's enough on him to hold him the rest of his crippled years. You did a job on his knee, Bonnie. Did you know there's a reward for him over in New Mexico? They've hauled him away in an extradition, and they can have him. He's one nasty piece of bad news."

He ambled over to the dining table, took off his hat, and accepted the mug Fergie was holding out to him.

"They mostly all had records, except the ones you may have come to know as Fenster, Griff, and Budge." Clayton sat down at the table as Bonnie slid a plate of biscuits and gravy in front of him and put down a napkin and silverware. "You'll take over the Bluebonnet Café one of these days, Bonnie."

"I've got my hands full cooking for this lot," she said, "and those two little boys there."

She waved a hand at Maury, who had just come up the stairs and was leading Little Al by the hand. Maury was twenty-plus years older than her, but she still spoke of him like he was a little boy.

"I understand you took out the one with the Uzi, Maury."

Maury grinned back at Clayton. "There won't be any charges for that, will there?"

"Nope. Like I said, those guys had records, and we have plenty more on them now. We have what's left of Moog Palance in the ground by now. You probably saw in the news how the feds took credit for raiding Semion Kashov's warehouse, thus solving quite a number of semi-truck cargo thefts."

He waved for Al to sit down at the table while he cut off a piece of biscuit and swabbed it through the gravy. "I'm curious why you suggested we take it easy on those two, Budge and Griff. We suspect Fenster has been a getaway man for a number of heists before being Moog's chauffeur. And he was driving a stolen vehicle. But you still could have pressed trespassing charges on Budge and Griff if you'd wanted to. They were on your property on and off enough times to be charged Airbnb rates."

"We have a feeling they aren't anything near the badasses of those others," Fergie said. "They had just fallen on hard times. And that big ol' Budge dude did save Bonnie and Little Al's lives. In fact, we kind of voted that if that reward for Brick gets paid out, that they should get it.

That kind of money might put them back on their feet and on a straight path. Sure, they may have a wrinkle or two in their past, but we think they might have good hearts that should be encouraged."

"I might could get on the same page with that. You got a card to play?" Clayton's eyes narrowed as he shoveled in another forkful and chewed.

"There's this." Al took a folded piece of paper out of his pocket and slid it over to Clayton. "I made a Xerox copy of the original log page, the only copy not destroyed by someone."

Clayton put down his fork and opened the page and was unsuccessful in hiding a grin. "Nelson. You can say the guy's damn name. We'd been like brothers for more than thirty years before he decided to run against me. You know, we might have lost the original if Meat Jenkins hadn't tipped me off about what building you'd been sniffing around in. The original logbook is safely locked in my safe now."

"What's going to happen to those two girls?" Fergie asked.

"Don't you know that when they heard from Klive that he was going to run their story, only with a different name for the abuser, they figured they probably weren't going to get paid by Nelson. The one they call Wacky Jacky had the brass to call me and ask if I was willing to pay what they'd been promised by him, on condition that they stay hushed. She admitted they knew all along it hadn't been me but it had been Nelson. 'But money's money, isn't it?' she said."

"And fraud is fraud," Fergie said. "They'd best hope you don't sue them both for all they're worth." She nearly said, "Which couldn't be much." But their own mean lives were enough punishment, having to live out their days as themselves.

Clayton nodded. "I told them that if they even think of trying to play that game, they should round up a lawyer pronto. You wouldn't believe the salty mouth on that gal."

"Oh yes, I would," Fergie said.

"So, Budge and Griff. What about them?" Al pressed again.

"I've already cut them loose. They were honest enough about what they were up to although, if they had found any gold from their tall tale, taking it off the property would have been theft. If you found it, you could keep it as long as it's on your place and not state land. They showed me the letter, and I've heard sillier motives for bad behavior. They even told me quite a bit more about their pasts than they needed to, kind of acting like I was a father confessor, stuff they needed to get off their chests if they were to start afresh. They've had some experiences, let me tell you, and a bit to be ashamed of. But they've learned a lot from all this. If you have no charges to press and feel they've redeemed themselves, then I'm with you. I gave them a stern life-coaching chat and got them both jobs, Griff at a clothing store and Budge in a bookshop. I've checked on them already, and their employers say they wish all their employees worked as avidly. They're to keep in touch about any possible reward money, which is more real than their gold ever was. I've got their commitment that they're going to testify against the others, and Moog, being dead now, is off their back about money. I even floated them a little up-front money to get by on until they get paid. In payment of a kind for the bother they caused by trespassing, they offered up the metal detector, which you all can keep. I understand Maury took a shine to it."

"Thanks," Bonnie said. "He was needing a new toy."

"I'll tell you something else that happened," Clayton said. "After I gave them each some money, the big one, Budge, said he'd like to give three hundred dollars back to go to a little old lady they'd burgled. He gave me the location. It was the home of Francis Sullivan, a retired gal who lived alone and had reported a burglary. She had said she was just glad her little dog, Chico, hadn't been hurt. That told me a lot about the big guy's chances of making a fresh, clean start though he had certainly made some mistakes. One cleared up a long-ago incident at a kicker bar we'd never figured out. The victim there turned out to be a guy who we knew had been robbing other dancing patrons on a regular basis, but we hadn't been able to catch him. So, justice wise, that was a wash and self-defense at that since the guy was robbing Griff."

"And?" Al asked, having seen something of a suppressed glitter in Clayton's eyes. He knew the man that well.

"Don't you know that when the big one wasn't there, the smaller one, Griff, did the same thing. He said to see that the old gal got four hundred dollars. That made me really believe that there might well be hope for him as well. He was the one about whom I had the most doubt of transitioning to a normal life. I think his experiences with real hardened criminals who would snuff him out as soon as look at him gave him a sterner lesson than anything I could have ever said."

He stood from the table. "I appreciate the breakfast, the chance to chat, and all you folks did on my behalf. But though it's Sunday and my so-called day off, you know I'm only a phone call away from having to rush back to the office if there's some sort of doodah of any kind going on in a county this populous, especially when visible action means votes and me staying in for one more term."

"Well, you have our votes," Fergie said.

"And you have my unflagging appreciation." Clayton put his hat back on and headed for the door.

AS THE HOUSE GOT QUIET that night, after Tanner went off with Al and Fergie into their bedroom, Bonnie tucked Little Al into his bed. She zipped the baby crib tent shut to keep him from roaming and turned to see Maury picking up the metal detector from the corner.

"It was nice of Clayton to let you keep that toy. But you can play with it in the morning, unless you want to check to see if I still have fillings in my teeth. Now, come to bed." She started to unbutton her blouse.

Maury grinned and flipped on the switch of the metal detector. He took a few steps while sweeping its search coil back and forth across the floor near the door. Even with the headset hanging to one side, the gadget suddenly made an enormously loud target signal.

Bonnie's mouth opened as wide as Maury's.

He turned it off and on again and got the same thing, which sounded as loud as World War Seven in the confines of the basement. Little Al let out a squawk, so Maury flipped off the power switch.

"Do you think we've found it, that cache of gold?" Bonnie put a hand inside the crib's tent to calm their boy.

"If so, we may well have set up Little Al's college fund. Since this is on private property and not state-owned land, I do believe we get to keep it."

"Now the big question," Bonnie said. "We've got to take a look. Do we dig right through the floor, or tunnel in from the outside edge of the slab?"

"Well, we were going to have to get a new rug anyway since you couldn't get every speck of the bloodstains out of this one. I think, if this turns out to be what we hope and expect, that we might be able to afford a new rug as well as patch up any hole we cut in the slab."

About the Author

Russ Hall lives on the north shore of Lake Travis near Austin, TX. An award-winning writer of mysteries, thrillers, westerns, poetry, and nonfiction books, he has had more than thirty-five books published, as well as numerous short stories and articles. He has also been on *The New York Times* bestseller list multiple times with co-authored non-fiction books, such as: *Do You Matter: How Great Design Will Make People Love Your Company* (Financial Times Press, 2009) with Richard Brunner, former head of design at Apple, and *Identity* (Financial Times Press, 2012) with Stedman Graham, Oprah's companion.

He was an editor for over 35 years with major publishing companies, ranging from Harper & Row (now HarperCollins) to Simon & Schuster to Pearson. He has been a pet rescue center volunteer, a mountain climber, and a probable book hoarder who fishes and hikes in his spare moments.

Read more at www.russhall.com.

About the Publisher

Dear Reader,

We hope you enjoyed this book. Please consider leaving a review on your favorite book site.

Visit our site to find more quality books!

Read more at https://RedAdeptPublishing.com.